His eye⬛⬛⬛⬛ steadily on hers.

'I admir⬛⬛⬛⬛⬛⬛⬛⬛t only beautif⬛⬛⬛⬛⬛⬛⬛ugh to turn any ⬛⬛⬛⬛⬛⬛t think you even realise th⬛⬛⬛⬛⬛yal and true. You'd never let anyon⬛⬛⬛uddenly his face looked grim as he added, 'Unusual in a woman. The ideal partner, in fact.'

Alice's face flamed and, putting up her hands to cool her cheeks, she said unsteadily, 'Most women are loyal and true. You shouldn't denigrate them like that.'

James's voice was bitter. 'I speak from experience. . .'

Mary Bowring was born in Suffolk, educated in a convent school in Belgium, and joined the WAAF during World War II, when she met her husband. She began to write after the birth of her two children, and published three books about her life as a veterinary surgeon's wife before turning to medical stories.

Recent titles by the same author:

VERSATILE VET
VET IN A QUANDARY
VETS IN OPPOSITION
VETS AT VARIANCE
VET IN CHARGE

VET WITH
A SECRET

BY
MARY BOWRING

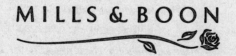

MILLS & BOON

MILLS & BOON, the Rose Device and
LOVE ON CALL are trademarks of the publisher.
Harlequin Mills & Boon Limited,
Eton House, 18-24 Paradise Road, Richmond, Surrey TW9 1SR

© Mary Bowring 1996

ISBN 0 263 79626 4

Set in Times 11 on 12 pt. by
Rowland Phototypesetting Limited
Bury St Edmunds, Suffolk

03-9607-42089

Made and printed in Great Britain

CHAPTER ONE

ALICE NORTON, MRCVS, sighed with relief as she shut the garage doors and checked that the surgery was locked and secure. It had been a long, hard day. Bracing herself, she forced a smile as she went through the passageway into the kitchen of the large old house.

Her mother looked up from stirring a saucepan on the Aga.

'It's all ready,' she said and added cheerfully, 'I'm expert at keeping meals hot. After all, I had years of experience with your father being called out at all hours.'

For a moment her smile faded and Alice felt a pang as she shared the sense of loss they both felt. She said quickly, 'We must get a microwave. It would make things much easier for you.' Then as she glanced at the table her eyes widened. 'Wine, too? Goodness! What are we celebrating?'

Her mother took the lid off the fragrant casserole and gave a wry smile.

She said slowly, 'We're celebrating the fact that, this evening, we are going to make a firm decision with regard to our future.' She paused, then, as Alice began to demur, she added, 'No, darling— you can't go on like this. You look dead tired. I'm getting very concerned about the load of work you have taken on since your father's death. On duty twenty-four hours a day.'

She drew a long breath then went on slowly, 'I know that before he became ill the two of you managed very well but now you're trying to do the impossible.'

Alice's beautiful grey eyes looked troubled but she shook her head. 'Not impossible. Difficult, I admit, but I'm coping.' She was silent for a few minutes, then she shrugged, 'Well, to be honest, I am finding it more and more difficult. It's the large animal work. The farmers get impatient. They don't like being kept waiting if they want me when I'm in the middle of an operation or I have a busy surgery.'

She stopped, seeing the shadow in her mother's face. Bracing herself, she said briskly, 'Let's have some wine. Perhaps it will help us to sort things out.'

Later, beside the fire in the living room, Mrs Norton said, 'Let's go over the various options. First, we could sell the practice—lock, stock and barrel. This house with its surgery annexe, the goodwill and so on. That would mean—'

'I know only too well what it would mean,' Alice said bitterly. 'I would have to get a job as assistant in another practice well away from this area.' Her voice softened. 'I'm sure you would never complain but I also know you love this place with its memories of Dad and all your married life. So let's put that idea aside and consider another one.'

'Getting in an assistant to do the farm work? That shouldn't be too difficult.'

Alice frowned. 'It shouldn't be but I haven't had any luck so far. That advertisement I put in the *Veterinary Record* yielded five answers. All men, of course, but as soon as they realised that they would be working for a woman they lost interest. And if a woman applies it wouldn't help with the farmers. You know how chauvinistic they are.'

'True,' Mrs Norton sighed. 'Well, so far as I can see, it comes back to selling up. I'll get myself a little flat and leave you free to work where you like.'

'But this is where I like,' Alice protested. 'I want to build up Dad's practice to what it used to be—a nice family mixed practice. I feel—' She stopped as the telephone rang.

Picking it up, she listened carefully. Then she said drily, 'No. The position is not yet filled. I've had several replies from men who seemed quite suitable but as soon as they learnt I was the owner of this practice they didn't want to know any more. Their masculine pride found it unacceptable to work for a woman.'

An unmistakable male chuckle came over the receiver, causing Mrs Norton who was listening intently to sit up in surprise. She waited patiently while the conversation continued and when at last Alice replaced the telephone she held her curiosity in check, not wishing to receive another disappointment.

But Alice's face was alight as she sat down again.

'This may be an answer to our problem. This

man—he has had several years of experience in mixed practice and is now looking for somewhere to settle down and put his plate up. That will take some time so he says he could come here for six months.'

'Why only six months?'

'Oh, didn't I say? Well, he's just come over from Australia where his father is a vet and is now staying for six months or thereabouts with his brother who lives not far from here. Seeing my advertisement, he thought he would like to work during this stay with his brother.'

'Hmm!' Mrs Norton looked dubious and Alice stared at her.

'What's wrong with that?'

'Oh, nothing really.' Mrs Norton paused then said slowly, 'It just seems odd that he should take on a full-time job while he's staying with his brother. Not much time for enjoying himself.'

'Well—' Alice shrugged '—I expect he'll explain everything tomorrow, though actually I don't think it's our business.' She paused. 'He's coming here immediately after morning surgery. Then if he proves suitable he can come out with me and get an idea of the farm work.'

She fell silent, staring into the fire and looked so tired that her mother's heart was wrung with pity. Her lovely daughter, only twenty-four and already burdened with worry. She should be enjoying her youth and with her almost astonishing beauty she could have had a wonderful social life.

Sighing, Mrs Norton studied the slim figure,

the rich dark hair with its auburn lights, the straight brows over clear grey eyes fringed by long black lashes and the full generous mouth lifted now in a half-smile as she pondered the good news she had just received. A sudden thought came to Mrs Norton and she said,

'Supposing you get another applicant who is willing to come permanently? What will you do then?'

Alice frowned. 'Well, that would be a bit awkward, wouldn't it?' She shrugged. 'I'll cross that bridge if and when I come to it. Personally, I don't think it's likely.' She thought for a moment. 'I'll warn him anyhow.'

She fell silent again, recalling how she had liked the sound of his voice. Deep and sympathetic with a hint of humour—a pleasant colleague who would help her overcome her present depression.

Surgery the next morning was mostly routine, with the exception of a difficult client who seemed unable to accept or even understand the advice she was given as to the future welfare of her tremendously overweight cat. At last, refusing to follow the dietary instructions, she gathered up her unfortunate pet, declaring that her Minnie was in reality a very small eater just as she herself was.

Squeezing her large bulk through the doorway, she pushed against a young man who stood back politely to let her pass before walking into the surgery.

Smiling, he said, 'Am I too early? I'm James Preston—your caller of last night.'

Giving him an answering smile, Alice quickly

summed him up—tall and broad-shouldered, hair nearly as dark as her own and a tanned rather stern face lightened by clear blue eyes. The expression in those eyes was one of admiration as he, in his turn, studied her quite openly.

Seated opposite him in her office she felt strangely nervous. It was a new experience for her to interview an applicant and this man seemed more self-confident than she was. At last he broke the silence.

'First of all I'll give you my qualifications and the experience I've already had. It's fairly extensive but, as I told you on the phone, I haven't taken on anything permanent so far.'

She listened attentively and became more and more certain that he measured up to her requirements. About his personal life he was slightly more reserved but when he mentioned where he was staying she exclaimed,

'Fairlands Farm? We—my father and I—always did the animals there but I haven't been called in since it was sold. I assumed that the new owner had gone to another vet.'

'I think you'll find that my brother will continue as your client. He's very anxious to succeed as a farmer. He's more or less starting from scratch, though, because the original herd was sold before the farmhouse was put up for sale.' Suddenly he grinned. 'And, of course, if you take me on as your assistant I'll twist his arm if he dares to contemplate any other vet.'

She laughed. 'Is he older than you?'

'Yes. He's thirty-five to my thirty. Married to

a nice girl. Two children—a boy and a girl.' He paused. 'However, you can't be all that interested in my relations so suffice it to say that you won't have to bother about accommodation. I can stay with them—that's if you take me on.'

He stopped and there was silence for a few moments. At last he added thoughtfully, 'I gather from what you've told me that you are trying to build up this practice to what it was in your father's time. That's a tough assignment because you have the disadvantage of being a woman vet.'

Alice frowned. 'That's a sexist remark, isn't it?'

'I suppose it sounds like that but—' He shrugged. 'I don't mean it in a derogatory sense. You know very well that as regards farm work—'

'Of course I know,' she said irritably. 'That's why I want a male assistant. I want to keep those wavering clients because if they leave me I'll never get them back again.'

James nodded thoughtfully. 'Best thing you can do, but I'm afraid I can only offer you six months' work. If you take me on you'll have to continue your search for a permanent assistant.'

'I realise that—' she smiled at him '—but it's getting urgent and you've come just in the nick of time. So let's get down to terms.'

They had just made the necessary arrangements when the telephone rang. Answering it, Alice listened, then said calmly,

'Yes, of course I can manage it. I'll be right over.' Replacing the instrument, she turned to James. 'A calving case that has defeated the herdsman. So it will be a difficult one.' She laughed drily, 'I'm sure Mr Bailey will be delighted to see a male vet. He thinks the job will be too much for me.'

'It might well be if it has defeated the herdsman. It usually means that the calf is lying in the wrong position and that does require a lot of strength—more than you possess, in spite of your medical knowledge.' His eyes swept over her, then, looking up, he met her resentful gaze. He grinned. 'I'm right, aren't I?'

She shrugged. 'Yes, of course, and in the old days my father would have done a job like this. Mind you, I did do quite a lot of farm work and the farmers accepted me.' She laughed ruefully. Probably because they knew Dad was in the background.' She got up. 'We'd better go.'

A great sense of relief filled Alice as she settled herself behind the wheel of her car. For the time being her problem was solved and the fact that James would be lodging with his brother made the whole thing easier than she had expected. She drew a long, relaxed breath and James looked at her curiously.

'What's wrong? Are you regretting your decision already?'

Alice laughed. 'No. Of course not. You've lifted a great burden off my shoulders.' She wanted to say that she wished he could stay on in a permanent position but it was too soon. After all, she had to test his aptitude for farm work and his reliability in general.

Instead, she asked casually, 'What do you contemplate doing when you've done your six months

here? Will you perhaps go back to Australia—
work in your father's practice?'

'No. Australia has too many unhappy memories
for me. If it wasn't for the fact that my father has
settled there I would never go back at all.'

Surprised at his sudden bitterness, she shot him
a quick glance and saw that he was looking grim
as he stared ahead. Quickly suppressing a strong
desire to probe further, she lapsed into silence
until they reached the farm. Then she turned to
him. 'I'll tell Mr Bailey that you are coming to
work with me and hand over the calving to you.'

Suddenly she exclaimed, 'Goodness! Your
obstetric gown and boots—I've only got my own
things in the car.'

'That's OK. I transferred my things into your
boot while you were closing the garage doors.'

'That was quick thinking.' She smiled at him
and met a look that was so companionable that
her heart warmed to him. Resourceful and quietly
practical—what a blessing he was going to be.

Mr Bailey was, as she had guessed, delighted
to meet a male vet and led them to the exhausted
cow. A brief consultation, an internal examination, and James got to work. It took half an hour
and by that time even he was tired. Rubbing his
right arm ruefully he looked down at the calf.

'A fine little heifer,' he said, 'and not damaged
at all in spite of her struggle to get into this world.'

The mother turned her head and nudged her
offspring and in a minute the calf was feeding. The
little group standing around watched in silence for
a while, then James said,

'It's always moving, isn't it—the miracle of birth?'

Alice nodded in sympathy but the farmer laughed. 'I'm afraid I'm a bit blasé. I think in monetary terms.' He turned to Alice. 'Am I going to be charged extra for having two vets here?'

She laughed. 'Of course not. Mr Preston did all the work and, in fact, is taking over all the farm work in the practice, so I would be glad if you would pass that on among your friends.'

On the way back to the car her pang of regret at handing over the large animals was soon followed by a sense of relief that she had taken the first step towards the rebuilding of her father's practice.

James broke the silence. 'You must come and meet my brother and his wife. He's got about six hundred acres, mostly arable, but once he's built up his herd he'll be quite a good client.'

'That will be interesting,' Alice said, then added, 'When you finally settle down I suppose you'll want to be within easy reach of each other?'

He made no answer and Alice got the impression that she was being rebuffed. She shrugged to herself. Perhaps he had a problem that would take time to resolve. She must remember not to pry too deeply. Meantime, she must be content to have her own problem solved for the present and for that she was thankful.

Her mother was in the surgery when they arrived and once introductions were made Mrs Norton said,

'You've arrived in the nick of time.' She

laughed. 'We were nearly on the point of selling up the house and practice.'

James looked taken aback. 'Surely that would have been unnecessarily drastic? You could have let the farm work go and concentrated on small animals.'

Alice nodded. 'Yes, I could have done that but this has always been a mixed practice and I want to keep it this way.'

There was a short silence and then Mrs Norton said,

'Will you have some lunch with us? Nothing special but I make quite a good omelette. We have our own hens.'

'I'd enjoy that very much—' James smiled gratefully '—but please don't think you have to feed me. I'll get a pub lunch in the ordinary way and have dinner with my brother and his wife.'

It was a pleasant meal enlivened by a bottle of wine from her father's stock. Alice said, 'Just to celebrate your arrival,' and showed him the label. 'Australian—rather appropriate.'

He studied the name and suddenly he went pale. 'Quite a coincidence,' he said coolly. 'I know the family who run that vineyard. In fact, my fiancée—my ex-fiancée, I should say—was the daughter of the house.' He added drily, 'I must say I'm surprised their wine has found popularity in this quiet part of England.'

There were a few moments of embarrassed silence before Mrs Norton took up his last phrase.

'We're not as backward as all that here in Sussex, you know. If you have the time you can get plenty of sophisticated entertainment in the coastal towns. And, of course, it's easy to get over to France. That should appeal to an Australian.'

James shook his head. 'I'm not an Australian. My brother and I were born and brought up with our parents in Shropshire. Then my father had a sudden urge to up sticks and live in what he called a better climate. He put up his plate in Perth, Western Australia, and that was that. But my brother and I both pined for England so as soon as we were able we returned.'

Suddenly, quite abruptly, he changed the conversation and Alice found herself being questioned about her practice and, in particular, about the lack of a veterinary nurse. She shrugged ruefully.

'That's a sore point at the moment. Before my father's death we had a qualified VN but she had to leave and look after her sick mother. So my mother—' she smiled as she glanced lovingly at Mrs Norton '—took over and has managed very satisfactorily.' She sighed. 'Perhaps soon we'll be able to engage another nurse but that's a problem for the future.'

James nodded. 'It's the old thing, isn't it? Veterinary wives—what would vets do without them?'

'Does your mother help your father in his surgery?' Mrs Norton asked and Alice saw a shadow pass over James's face and realised that once more, the talk was getting too personal for his liking. He said briefly, 'She used to before her death but now I have a stepmother and she isn't interested in animals.'

Longing to ask more questions but deterred by the closed look on James's face, Alice glanced at her mother. She too must have felt the tension in the atmosphere but she was at her most tactful, and commented,

'It would be a very dull world if we were all alike, wouldn't it?' to which James responded with a short laugh.

Evidently, Alice thought, the trouble lay in his father's second marriage. A very ordinary reaction and of no importance to anyone but himself.

She was intrigued, however, by his mention of an ex-fiancée. He had said she was 'the daughter of the house' as though she had since left home. Perhaps that was the answer to his apparent reluctance to discuss his personal life. She shrugged. Natural enough, surely. Later, perhaps, when they knew each other better, she would learn more.

Soon James Preston had become an integral part of the practice, so smoothly had he fitted in to the daily routine. The farmers had welcomed him and he was proving himself to be very competent.

Then one morning he came in at the end of a quiet surgery, asked Alice if she had any operations to do and when she shook her head suggested that she come with him to meet his brother and sister-in-law.

'I rather think I shall have to put their old dog to sleep. They've put it off as long as possible but now—' he looked sad '—it really must be done.'

They decided to go in James's car and Alice's mother promised to hold the fort, as she put it smilingly.

Spring had been late in arriving but at last it seemed to have made up its mind. As they went outside Alice drew a long breath of delight. A blue sky, the trees in their delicate early green and in the distance the lovely, echoing call of the first cuckoo. Getting into the car Alice smiled at James.

'Isn't that the loveliest sound? It always gives me a thrill whenever I hear it.'

He nodded, his eyes fixed on her. 'Yes, it's beautiful. And this is a perfect day for me. England in springtime, a lovely girl beside me— what more could a man wish for?'

His words were so obviously sincere that her colour rose as she met the open admiration in his steady gaze and she felt a strange thrill that had nothing to do with the cuckoo. Then, almost as though he regretted his impulsive speech, he said briskly, 'Let's get on, shall we?'

Ten minutes later he pulled up at the gate leading up to a large farmhouse. 'Here we are. It's a nice house, isn't it?'

'Yes. I know it of old. As I told you, my father used to do the farm work in the former owner's time.'

'It's a bit run-down now but David has plans to do it all up eventually. Sophie, his wife, is full of plans but she has her hands full with their two children and the animals they are gradually accumulating. David is determined to make the farm pay although things are pretty difficult these days.'

'Oh, I don't know,' Alice shrugged. 'What with subsidies for "set aside" land and growing certain crops I don't think farmers are doing too badly.' She paused. 'What has your brother been doing up till now? I gather he's new to farming.'

'He's a chartered surveyor—well, he's out of it now but his experience will always be useful in this new life he's chosen.'

Alice looked thoughtful. 'He's taken a risk, hasn't he? Let's hope he doesn't come unstuck, for his family's sake.'

James laughed. 'He's got nothing to worry about. Our mother left us both enough to be comfortable even without working.

'I'm not saying that's necessarily a good thing— it's a bit unsettling. That's what it's done for me, anyway. I've looked around and found nothing to satisfy me. But at last I've taken myself in hand. Given myself six months in which to make a final decision.' He paused and shrugged. 'That's what I tell myself anyway. I can't continue doing nothing—it's demoralising.'

He opened the car, went to the gate, swung it open and came back. Once in the drive he got out again to shut the gate and as he settled himself in the car again he said, 'The truth is I love veterinary work and have come to realise that I don't ever want to do anything else. The legacy from my mother unsettled me at first but now I've got used to it and decided to take it in my stride.

'Which means—' he turned to grin at her '—I can practise as a vet without the usual financial worries that go with our profession.'

Alice looked at him thoughtfully. 'You should be a very happy man.'

'Happy? Ah, that's a different thing altogether. Ever since—' He stopped, drew a long breath, then said harshly, 'I don't think I'll ever be quite happy again.'

Impulsively Alice said, 'Why ever not?' but he shrugged dismissively and she knew she had been too curious.

Suddenly he pointed ahead and Alice saw a girl coming down the drive towards them. She said, 'Is that your sister-in-law?'

'Good Lord, no,' he said with a grin. 'Much too slim for Sophie. It's Becky Sinclair—the farm secretary. That's not a very demanding job so she helps out occasionally with the animals. My brother says she is a treasure. She's a nice girl. Lives in one of the farm cottages—we passed it as we turned into the drive.'

Leaning out of the open window, he called to her and Alice studied her as she approached. Wearing boots and a waterproof jacket and her short hair blown in the breeze, she presented an attractive picture.

As she leant forward to shake hands when James introduced her, Alice met a look from green eyes that were far from friendly. For some reason, it seemed that Becky Sinclair resented seeing another girl seated in James's car. She smiled to herself. A clear case of jealousy and rather obvious at that.

She wondered if James was aware of the fact that Becky only had eyes for him. Probably not, for as she turned away, saying, 'See you again soon,' he made no reply but began talking of Sophie.

'I expect she'll have laid on an enormous lunch for us. How's your appetite?'

Alice laughed. 'Well, not huge but I'll do my best.'

Sophie was kind and welcoming. A plump, pretty mother figure who quickly made Alice feel at ease and her husband, David, who soon joined her, was equally friendly. An older version of James though not, she decided, quite as good-looking.

He laughed as his wife led them towards the large, flagstoned kitchen and said, 'We do have a formal dining room but somehow we always end up here.'

He sighed then and added sadly, 'I'm afraid there's a reason for it today.' Pointing to a black Labrador lying in a large dog-bed near the Aga, he added, 'He's fourteen now, very blind, bumps into things and has lost interest in everything. We've given him a good life but he's no longer happy.' He turned to James. 'Will you do the necessary?'

James was silent for a moment then said slowly, 'I'd rather leave it to Alice. She does all the small animals. I'll go and get the necessary from my car. Shan't be long.'

Bending down to stroke the old dog, Alice felt resentful. James should not have given her this sad task, especially on this her first visit to his family. But his brother and sister-in-law accepted his decision calmly and Sophie bent down, kissed the dog's head and whispered a few last loving words, looking up as James returned.

It was soon done. There was no reaction to the injection and as they watched the slow breathing gradually cease there was a general feeling of release at the merciful ending to a long, happy life. When at last David wrapped up the quiet body in a towel and took it outside, saying that he would bury him later, Sophie wiped her eyes and said,

'The children are spending the day with friends. I've prepared them a little and I'll tell them more when I fetch them later.' After a moment she continued, 'In a few weeks' time I'll look around for a puppy to console them.' Tears gathered in her eyes again. 'It'll take a lot to console me, however.'

During lunch the conversation was mostly about farming and when, after coffee, David took James out to look at the animals Alice declined his offer to accompany them and settled down with Sophie to a second cup of coffee.

Suddenly she realised that Sophie was gently drawing her out with kindly questions about her personal life. It was relaxing to be able to discuss her problems since her father's death and her worries about the future of the practice. At last she sat back and sighed.

'So you see how relieved I was to find just the help I needed from James.'

Sophie looked at her thoughtfully. 'You say he has limited his time with you to six months. Do you know why?' Alice told her what James had given as his reason and, to her surprise, Sophie looked sceptical.

At last she said, 'He was badly shaken when his mother and his fiancée were killed in a car accident. Then, to make matters worse, his father got married again very quickly. That caused a rift between them.'

Alice's eyes widened. 'How awful! No wonder he can't settle down.'

Sophie smiled wryly. 'Well, David has managed to take it in his stride but, of course, it was worse for James, especially as the accident was his fiancée's fault.' She hesitated for a moment. 'Don't let on that I've told you. James refuses to talk about it even to us.'

She finished her coffee and added thoughtfully, 'We're hoping he'll meet a nice girl eventually to help him recover. Someone like our farm secretary—Becky Sinclair. A lovely girl, we think, but so far our matchmaking efforts haven't met with any success.'

She glanced out of the window, and said, 'They're coming back.' She smiled at Alice and added ruefully, 'I've let my tongue run away with me as usual. Still, I'm sure you'll keep it all to yourself, won't you?'

Alice nodded. 'Of course I will,' she said, and looked up as the two men came into the room.

David was laughing as he pointed to his brother.

'The great advantage of having a vet in the family. Belinda—our sow—has had a litter of twelve but her milk has failed. I was very worried but James has worked a miracle. One injection behind her ear and the milk came down in a few minutes. The piglets are celebrating—getting quite exhilarated.'

Sophie looked puzzled. 'Behind the ear? Why there?'

'It's about the only place to get a needle through that thick skin,' James said calmly and Sophie laughed. 'I learn something new every day,' she said, then turning to Alice she added, 'You also do farm animals, don't you? That's useful—we'll have two vets to call on, won't we?'

James glanced quickly at Alice but said nothing so she replied, 'Well, I'll do your small animals—dogs, cats, children's pets and so on, but it would be best if you called on James for the farm animals. That's the general idea, anyway, but of course in an emergency we can always swop roles.'

Goodbyes were said, but as they were about to drive away Becky Sinclair walked up and waved them down. Ignoring Alice, she spoke to James. 'I've been thinking—I have an elderly dog. Will you look after her and do all the necessary injections and things?'

'Well.' James looked embarrassed. 'Actually, I'm not doing small animal work. That's Alice's field so—'

'But I want *you* to be my vet,' Becky interrupted and turned to Alice. 'You can make an exception in my case, can't you?'

Alice hesitated but James said firmly, ''Fraid not, Becky. I must stick to my agreement with Alice. It's a straightforward arrangement and saves a lot of confusion.'

'That's absurd!' Becky's voice was needle-sharp. 'You live here. Suppose I had an emergency with Cora in the middle of the night. Am I supposed to wait until your—er—employer turns up?'

There was a moment's awkward silence before Alice said smoothly, 'Of course not. Naturally, emergencies are different.' She paused and, anxious to dispel the antagonism which seemed to have arisen between them, she smiled and turned to James. 'I think we'd better make an exception in Becky's case. You can look after her Labrador. That's if you agree.'

He frowned and said stiffly, 'If you insist.' Turning to Becky, he added coldly, 'Of course I'll have to charge you like any other client.'

'Naturally.' There was a small note of triumph in Becky's voice. 'I'm glad you understand.' Ignoring Alice, she gave James a beaming smile and walked on up the drive.

There was silence as they continued their journey and Alice smiled wryly to herself. Becky's motive was very clear and she felt well and truly snubbed. Then suddenly James said resentfully, 'Why on earth did you give in like that?'

She glanced at him in surprise. 'Well, there wasn't much option, was there?'

'You could have stuck to your guns—said that

was the way we worked and that she could get someone else if she didn't like it.'

'Oh, don't be silly. Why should I lose a client for the sake of a hastily thought out arrangement? Anyway, why do you mind? Don't you like Becky?'

His voice was cold. 'That's not the point. The truth is that I don't want—' He shrugged indifferently. 'Well, as you say, it's not important, after all.'

That seemed to be that but Alice was puzzled. He had broken off in the middle of a phrase that seemed to hold a hidden meaning. What was it that he didn't want? To get involved with Becky? To get involved with any girl? Had the tragedy of his fiancée's death left a scar that was still not healed?

Perhaps he felt he was being pressurised by his brother and sister-in-law who, though well meaning, didn't understand that it was too soon for him to love again.

CHAPTER TWO

THE slight disagreement over Becky's Labrador soon died down but there were other occasions when the arrangement could not be adhered to too rigidly.

Most of the farmers were well pleased with James but a few expressed their regret that Alice seemed to have given up large animal work. To these she replied that she was still available if James was busy elsewhere.

She was pondering the situation one morning when James walked into the surgery. It was a cold day with a biting east wind and he went over to the radiator and stood warming his hands for a few moments before saying,

'Had a call before breakfast. Valley Farm—difficult calving, but I managed to get the calf out in the end. Mr Thompson was pleased. Sent his regards to you and informed me I was nearly as good as you so there's one farmer who remains faithful.' He paused. 'Any coffee going?'

'Of course.' She got up and put on the kettle. 'I must say I should miss the farm work if I had to give it up entirely.'

'Guessed you would,' James said as he sat down at the table. 'In fact I've given the matter some thought. For my part I'd like to do some small

27

animal work. It might be a good idea to rethink our first arrangement.'

She turned to the boiling kettle and, once she'd filled the mugs, he got up and carried them to the table. Sitting opposite him, she said thoughtfully, 'I think you're right. After all when you leave here—' She left the phrase unfinished but he took her up quickly.

'That's another thought I've had.' He drank slowly while Alice's heart missed a beat. Was he going to cut short his six months' agreement? Then she calmed herself. He wouldn't leave her in the lurch like that. She looked at him searchingly and saw that he was smiling.

'I know what you're thinking. Don't worry. Of course I'll stay for six months. I don't break promises.

'However, I have a suggestion: I would like to settle here—put money into the practice by buying an equal-share partnership. I could get myself a house and buy all the latest equipment to bring the practice up to date. I haven't thought it all out yet and, of course, if you don't like the idea you have only to say.'

Stunned, she stared at James in silence. She felt she ought to jump at his offer yet she hesitated. Instinctively she drew back. It was too early to enter into such a commitment. At last she found her voice.

'Well—it's a most attractive offer—' She stopped, then added lamely, 'It requires thinking over. A lot of thinking, in fact.' She paused again. 'You've only been here a few weeks. You hardly know me and I don't really know you at all. Shall we decide when we get nearer to the end of your six months?'

'OK,' he said calmly. 'Suits me. But I shan't change my mind. As for not knowing you—you're wrong there.'

His eyes fixed steadily on hers, he added slowly, 'I admire you tremendously. You're not only beautiful—and God knows you're enough to turn any man's head, though I don't think you even realise that—but you're loyal and true. You'd never let anyone down.' Suddenly his face looked grim as he added, 'Unusual in a woman. The ideal partner, in fact.'

Her face flamed and, putting up her hands to cool her cheeks, she said unsteadily, 'Most women are loyal and true. You shouldn't denigrate them like that.'

His voice was bitter. 'I speak from experience, whereas you—' He shook his head slowly. 'I'm embarrassing you. So back to my suggestion. This practice of yours is just what I'm looking for. It merely needs a bit more up-to-date equipment.' He glanced up quickly and caught her frown. 'Don't look like that. You know you'll have to face up to this problem sooner or later. You also need a full-time veterinary nurse—your mother would welcome that I'm sure. She could always stand in when the nurse was off-duty.'

She avoided his steady gaze. 'You're right on all counts and eventually I hope to get all these things. But an equal partnership—it wouldn't be my practice any more.'

'What do you mean?' He frowned, then smiled wryly. 'You mean you don't want to share? You prefer to be a one-man—sorry—one-woman practice?'

Alice shrugged and nodded reluctantly. 'Just as my father was.'

'But he wasn't. You worked for him. Two vets.'

'That's why I advertised for an assistant. Not for a partner.'

'I see.' His voice was scornful. 'Not much future for him!'

She stiffened. James was making her look foolish by holding her plans up to ridicule. And that, she told herself, was how it would be if they entered into partnership. He would take complete charge. She would no longer be independent. She said calmly, 'Well, as I said, it's too soon to decide.'

Another thought came into her mind. 'You yourself might think differently. After all, why should you want to sink your money into someone else's practice when you could very well set up on your own?'

Then, with a strong desire to return his mocking criticism, she said scornfully, 'You might well meet a girl you would like to marry but who wanted to live in another part of the country.' She saw his face change. His mouth tightened and his eyes grew cold but she went ahead as yet other thought struck her.

'Perhaps I can guess the reason why you would like to settle here. According to your sister-in-law Becky would make the ideal wife for you. And why not? I should think she'd be just right.'

She drew a long breath, picked up her coffee and drank deeply, watching him over the rim of the mug. Then, to her dismay, she saw his face whiten slowly. Hastily she said, 'Oh dear! I'm sorry. I shouldn't have said that.'

'No, you shouldn't. You have no right to bring my personal life into a business talk. Nor have you the right to gossip about me with my sister-in-law.' He paused. 'Well, that decides it. Please forget my offer. I'll stay here for six months and that's all.'

He got up, went into the dispensary to collect necessary refills for his case then went out to his car.

Alice found herself shaking as she tried to sort out her thoughts. She had obviously gone too far and regretfully she recognised the justification for James's anger. Maybe she ought to apologise, though she doubted if he would forgive her. She sighed, finished her coffee and was washing the mugs when her mother walked in. 'I've just seen James. Is there anything wrong? He looked a bit grim.'

Alice hesitated. 'Nothing much. He had some suggestions for the practice to which I couldn't agree. You know, new equipment to bring it up to date. Expensive ideas.'

Her mother looked thoughtful. 'Your father was thinking along those lines. Don't you remember?'

'Yes, of course I remember but that was when the practice was thriving. Then he became ill and things have gone down since then.'

'Well, they're looking up now. Perhaps soon you'll be able to follow James's advice.' She paused. 'Ah, there's the phone.'

Picking up the receiver Alice was thankful that she had escaped having to give any further explanation and listened to an agitated caller. Replacing the telephone, she turned quickly to her mother.

'A dog hit by a car. It'll be here in a few minutes. I gather it's pretty serious.'

Everything was ready when the patient arrived but Alice's heart sank when she examined the black Labrador and lifted the front right leg which hung limply with no apparent injury. She looked up at the anxious owner.

'She's badly shocked and bruised, of course. I can help her there but this—' She shook her head. 'No power there at all. I'll X-ray her but it's quite obvious what has happened. The radial nerve is completely crushed. She can't even lift the limb— can only drag it along the ground. There's nothing I can do about that at present.'

She paused for a moment. 'There's a fifty-fifty chance that the nerve will recover but it may well take about four to six months. The first sign of recovery will be if she gradually tries to carry the limb.' She looked sympathetic. 'I'm sorry, Mr Sanders.'

'And if nothing happens—what then?'

It was the question she dreaded but she answered steadily, 'I could amputate.'

'Oh, God! That's terrible. She'd never manage

with only three legs. It would be better to put her to sleep.'

'I don't agree.' Alice shook her head. 'Look, I've come across this before. I've got some photographs—my father had to take a leg off a Labrador like yours. Wait—I'll get the pictures.'

She hurried into the office and came back with a large envelope. 'Here—see—this dog had a cancerous growth on its right front leg and it was necessary to amputate right up to the shoulder. My father did this three years ago and these photos show before and after the operation.

'A month afterwards the dog was running about, jumping into the car and going out with the other two dogs when the owner went shooting. He said that the bitch never seemed to notice the lack of her fourth leg.'

She went on to say, 'And a friend of ours—a gamekeeper—told us he saw a deer with a front leg missing. It was probably born like that but it bounded away when it thought it was in danger.'

Mr Sanders looked down at his dog. 'My lovely Bess. What have I done to you? I should have had you on a lead. That car couldn't stop in time. He offered to pay for treatment but I told him there was no need. Bess is insured and in any case it's not the financial side I'm worried about.'

Alice said gently, 'Bess has a fifty-fifty chance of recovery so you must concentrate on that. She is already a little overweight so you must watch that. With no real exercise she will get fatter if you don't cut out the extra biscuits and treats.'

He went away reluctantly, promising to pick

Bess up when Alice had made sure that she was ready to return home. Alice sighed heavily as the door shut behind him.

'I do hope I don't have to put that dog to sleep. Mr Sanders doesn't look the type to wait patiently to see if the radial nerve recovers.'

Her mother nodded in agreement. 'What if he decides on amputation? Do you think you can do it?'

'Of course I can,' Alice said sharply. 'I'm a qualified surgeon, remember? You would never have questioned Dad's ability—why doubt mine?'

'Oh, dear!' Mrs Norton laughed ruefully. 'I'm sorry. It's sometimes difficult for me to realise that—well—' Her words trailed off and Alice shrugged away her irritation. It wasn't that she was ungrateful. Her mother was a great help and it was only occasionally that she failed to come up to the standard of a veterinary nurse.

One like Carol, who had worked for them for years—even before Alice had qualified. She had left them with great regret in order to look after her invalid mother. Suddenly a memory came back. That announcement in the local paper—Carol's mother had died over a month ago. With a rush of shame Alice recalled that she had never got down to a letter of condolence.

Quickly going into her office, she sat down to write the difficult letter. Biting the end of her pen, she was searching for appropriate words when she heard the surgery door open and a second later James came in.

Forgetting their previous disagreement, she

said, 'I'm writing a belated letter of condolence to our former veterinary nurse. Her mother died a few weeks ago and I've only just remembered. I feel terribly guilty. Carol worked for my father for years.' She went on slowly, 'She only left to look after her mother.'

'Do you think she might like to come back to you—that is, if she is free?'

'That's an idea.' Alice gazed down at her letter. 'Obviously I can't ask her in a letter of condolence but I could ask her to come and see me.' Then she frowned. 'Actually I'm not sure if I could afford to employ her.'

'Well, that's up to you.' His voice was cool. 'I'm afraid I can't advise you there. I'm only a temporary assistant.'

This oblique reference to their previous talk brought a flush to Alice's face and she turned back to her letter. But James showed no sign of leaving. Instead he said, 'I'm sorry to interrupt you but I've been asked to put a proposition to you.'

Alice looked up. 'A proposition? Surely not that partnership again?'

'Of course not—' his voice was dry '—but it's relevant to the veterinary nurse question. Remember Becky—my brother's farm secretary?'

Alice nodded and tried not to show her apprehension. Something unpleasant was coming and her fears were confirmed as he went on to explain. At last she said,

'Becky to work here? But surely she has a full-time job with your brother?'

'Actually, it's only part-time. She could give you four half-days a week. And, more to the point, she doesn't want to be paid. She's anxious to train as a veterinary nurse and she thought a few weeks' experience in this practice would put her on the right path.' He paused. 'Or even a few months.'

'"A few months"—I see. While you're here, in fact.' Alice tried to keep the sarcasm out of her voice and apparently she succeeded for James nodded.

'That's the idea. You might find her very useful. She could relieve you of a lot of paperwork and in the surgery I'm sure you'd find her very helpful. It would also take some of the burden off your mother's shoulders.'

'You've thought of everything, haven't you?'

This time he heard the displeasure in her reply and he said sharply, 'So you think I'm interfering, do you? Well, maybe it looks like that but as one colleague to another I'm interested in helping you. It would give you the opportunity of getting out to the occasional farm, save you the unpleasant task of cleaning up after operations and she could help you to hold difficult patients.'

There was no getting away from it. It seemed a good scheme and one she would be foolish to refuse. But it didn't take into account the fact that she didn't like Becky and she was pretty sure that the feeling was reciprocated. She drew a long breath. 'I don't know what to say. I'll have to think it over.

'In any case I'd have to pay her something. I

don't like being under an obligation and it would make it awkward if I had to tick her off sometimes.'

To Alice's enormous relief the ringing of the telephone put an end to any more discussion. Answering it, she listened for a short while before putting her hand over the receiver and turning to James.

'These people—old friends actually—want a full veterinary examination of a horse they are thinking of buying. Now my father always did these examinations and although I've seen it done many times I really—well, to be frank—I don't think I'm quite up to it. How are you on equine experience?'

James smiled. 'Don't worry. I was brought up with horses and in my father's practice I was always the one sent out to do these examinations. Have you got the necessary papers?'

She nodded. What a relief! Turning back to the telephone she made the necessary arrangements. That done, she said, 'These people are family friends or, perhaps, I should say "were" because we've rather lost touch with them. I feel rather guilty about that so I'll come with you. The stables where the horse is are only a couple of miles from where my friends live.'

Next morning they set off and almost immediately Alice began to regret agreeing to take only one car as no doubt her old friends would invite her back to their house and James would have to be included. Somehow she didn't want him to hear about her involvement with Edward. His sister Molly might well bring his name into the conversation and it would be difficult to hide her embarrassment.

Well, she would have to be careful, that was all. Maybe it wouldn't be too difficult. Edward was far away—probably married by now—so what on earth was she worried about?

Her thoughts flew back to the time when she had imagined herself in love with him and had thought her heart was broken when he had got engaged to another girl. She had been able to hide her grief but his mother had told her quite openly that she was disappointed in Edward's choice.

She had said sorrowfully, 'I had hoped that he and you—' and had obviously been incredulous when Alice had denied firmly that she had ever loved her son. It had been a matter of pride not to show her shock and misery at the time. But she had succeeded and, not being able to bear seeing him with his fiancée, she had gradually let her friendship with his sister lapse.

Now she knew that her feelings had really been a kind of infatuation and was only too thankful that she was still heart whole. She smiled to herself ruefully and met James's amused glance.

'I don't know what thoughts are passing through your mind but I'll give you a penny for them.'

She laughed. 'They were far away in the past—not even worth that tiny coin.'

He was silent for a moment, then he said quietly, 'You are a source of mystery to me. Very intriguing. I would very much like to penetrate that wall you have erected between yourself and the world.'

'Don't be silly,' she retorted, and added quickly, 'What's more, you mustn't stare at me like that. You'll have us in a ditch if you're not careful. I'm beginning to wish we were in separate cars.'

James laughed softly. 'Sorry. Still, I can think of worse things than being in a ditch with you.'

Colour flooded into her face but she merely said, 'Next turning on the right—my friends' house is just round the bend.'

Five minutes later they got out of the car to be greeted joyfully by Molly. It was a pleasant reunion and after James had been introduced it was arranged that they should vet the horse first and then return to the house and catch up with all the news.

The chestnut mare looked in good condition and Alice watched carefully as the vetting proceeded. First of all, James took out an ophthalmoscope and looked at the internal part of the animal's eyes, then opened her mouth and looked at her teeth. 'About six years old,' he said to the owner, who nodded agreement.

Then he looked round the sides of the mouth and under the chin, searching for sores or ulcers. Satisfied, he passed his hand down the mare's legs, pressing the tendons and bones. Next he examined the 'frog' which, he explained to Molly, was a sort of pad that acted as a cushion to absorb shock.

Finally he articulated the joints to see that there was no pain or roughness. After that he asked the owner to walk the mare up a hard bit of road and bring her back at a trot while he looked at its action and for possible signs of lameness.

He listened to the heart and then asked the owner to saddle up and ride at a canter for about fifteen minutes and directly she pulled up he listened to her heart and lungs while she was blowing hard. A final walk and trot to see if any stiffness had developed and then he turned to Alice, who handed him a long sheet of paper.

He showed it to Molly and explained that it was like two maps of a horse—one for each side and the front and back of the legs. 'I have to put the markings in red. That white blaze on her head, for instance, and any acquired scars.' A final walk and trot and the vetting was over.

Then James turned to Molly. 'Now, if something should occur between now and the time you take possession of this mare, anything—a cut on barbed wire, a sudden lameness—then this vetting would be out of date.' He glanced at Alice. 'OK?'

'Of course,' she smiled, appreciating the fact that he was acknowledging her seniority. From now on she resolved to undertake this procedure with the confidence gained from watching him carefully.

Once back at her house Molly said, 'You must come in for a drink to celebrate, not only the successful vetting but something else. A complete surprise. Guess what?'

Without waiting for an answer she blurted out, 'Edward has come back. Without any warning. He arrived yesterday. Mother is over the moon, of course, and I expect you'll be as pleased as I am. I must get some glasses. Shan't be a minute.' At the door she hesitated. 'By the way, he's not married. That fell through.'

Stifling a gasp at the meaningful look that Molly cast her, Alice was nevertheless unable to control the rush of colour to her face and, irritated, she turned away from James's interested glance. He said softly, 'I feel rather *de trop* here but there's not much I can do about it, short of going to sit in the car.'

She said sharply, 'Don't be silly. This is a friendly family. No need to feel awkward.'

His eyebrows rose. 'Why are you so apprehensive, then? Is it because of the return of the son of the house?'

She blinked. He was too perceptive. He must, she decided, be put in his place. She looked at him scornfully, 'Good grief! All this pseudopsychology of yours! You really ought to drop it. It's annoying.'

James opened his mouth to reply but was forestalled by the sudden entrance of Molly and her mother. The latter's face was wreathed in smiles and, as she enveloped Alice in an affectionate embrace, she said, 'You couldn't have come at a better time. Edward will be here in a minute. He's looking forward so much to meeting you again.'

Embarrassed, Alice forced herself to speak lightly. 'I've almost forgotten what he looks like. Actually, I'm more pleased at meeting you and Molly again.' Turning, she introduced James and Molly then drew her aside.

'You mustn't mind Ma—you know what a matchmaking mother she is. I'm pretty sure you're no longer interested in Edward and I'll make that very clear to him as soon as I can.'

'I'm sure there's no need to do that. He was never interested in me and I got him out of my system long ago.'

'I believe you,' Molly nodded sympathetically. 'You'll find him changed, though. He's very prosperous—big business—though I don't know much about it yet.' She turned as the door opened. 'Ah, here he is.'

Alice, very conscious of his mother's watching eyes, put out a hand as a tall man came towards her and said coolly,

'Good gracious, Edward! Is it really you? Either you've changed or I've completely forgotten what you look like.'

CHAPTER THREE

IT WAS a silent drive back. James seemed absorbed in his thoughts while Alice's mind was on the change that she had seen in Edward. Gone was the amusing, rather boyish, friend and in his place was a sophisticated, smooth man of the world who had gazed at her searchingly. He had certainly not liked her cool reception of his unexpected return.

She frowned as she remembered the quick invitation to dinner to 'talk over old times' and the way in which he had brushed aside her excuses. She had, however, been firm in her refusal but was defeated by Mrs Horsley who, just when they were leaving, had asked her to lunch on her next free day. Molly had joined in the pressing invitation and this time Alice had found it impossible to say no.

She sighed to herself at the prospect of complications and suddenly James broke the silence. 'Going to be a bit difficult for you, isn't it?'

Irritated by the way he had read her troubled thoughts, she asked sharply, 'What on earth do you mean?'

He laughed softly. 'It's obvious. Ex-boyfriend turns up. You show your reluctance to renew the old relationship but he is determined to overcome your objections and is aided and abetted by his mother and sister.'

She gasped indignantly and snapped, 'You're at it again. You seem to think you know more about me than I do myself. But you're wrong. "Old relationship"—there never was any relationship. We were a trio—Edward, Molly and myself—we went everywhere together.'

Glancing at him scornfully, she met his eyes. Then, as he turned back to concentrate on his driving, she felt a strange emotion. There had been something in his expression that made her regret her outburst.

She said quietly, 'I'm sorry. I didn't mean to snap your head off but, as you have probably found out by now, I lose my temper when you try to analyse me. How would you like it if I started trying to pry into your mind?'

James's voice was dry. 'You're welcome to try. What would you like to know?'

The question startled her and her immediate reaction was to tell him that she wasn't interested enough but she knew that wasn't true. There was a lot about him that intrigued her. All the same she felt instinctively that she must hold back her curiosity. She said calmly, 'Nothing, really. I already know that you are a good vet and very helpful to me. That's all I need to know.'

'Is that your attitude towards everybody?' Suddenly his voice was harsh. 'Do you think only of what use they can be to you?'

He turned his head to glance at her, then added more gently, 'No need to answer. I wouldn't believe you anyway if you said yes. You are not like that. You feel deeply but you're afraid of getting hurt so you're always on the defensive.' He stopped, adding with a grin, 'Now, don't get angry again. That terrible frown doesn't sit well on your beautiful face.'

Alice drew a long breath. 'In future I think we'll always travel in separate cars. You irritate me beyond measure.'

He said no more and as soon as they arrived back Alice went straight into the surgery, followed a minute later by James.

Mrs Norton was in the act of replacing the telephone and smiled with relief as they came in. 'That was Mr Shelley at Hill Farm. He wants you to do some pregnancy diagnoses tomorrow morning. I explained that you would have to do your surgery first so he agreed to keep the cows in till ten o'clock.'

Alice frowned. 'I'll have to ring him back. I can't possibly get there before ten-thirty at the earliest.'

She moved towards the telephone but James said quickly, 'I can take over. It would be a pity to upset what you call a "loyal" farmer. I'll fit in my own calls later.'

Alice shook her head. 'I don't think that's a good idea. I'd hate to make difficulties for Mr Shelley—a rare farmer who takes no notice of gender.'

Her mother shrugged. 'I can understand why they mostly prefer a male vet. It's a question of

physical strength.' She turned to James. 'That's
true, isn't it?'

'That's one of the reasons, though really that
shouldn't apply these days. Apart from extremely
difficult calvings there are not many occasions
where physical strength is all-important. There are
ways of avoiding even this but another reason
is that some farmers are surprisingly delicately
minded. They get embarrassed when a woman vet
has to go into intimate details about the sexual
lives of their animals.'

Mrs Norton burst out laughing. 'Now I've heard
everything! Farmers with delicate minds,
indeed—that's a new one on me!' She went to
the door, then turned to Alice and said, 'By the
way, there's a letter for you. I've put it on
your desk.'

In the office Alice picked up the letter,
recognised the handwritten address and felt a
pang of guilt that she had not yet posted her letter
to Carol. Then, as she began to read, she gave a
sigh of relief. Apparently her mother had done
the necessary and had included Alice in her letter
of condolence.

Reading on, her eyes widened with pleasure.
Just what she had hardly dared to hope. Carol
wanted to return to her old job if it was still free.

What was more—Alice picked up the letter
again—'Now, I know that times must be hard for
you since your father's death so I don't want my
old salary. Much, much less. In fact I'll come
for nothing, if necessary. My mother has left me
comfortably off but I need to be occupied and I'd

rather work for you than anyone else. I could easily get a small flat near you so that would solve the accommodation question.'

Alice sent up a prayer of thankfulness. Now she could refuse that offer from Becky with a clear conscience. Jubilantly she went in search of James.

He listened carefully, smiled at Alice's delight at having her old friend back and promised to explain everything to Becky. Then, thoughtfully, he added, 'Of course, it may be some time before—what's her name—Carol is able to get fixed up. Why not let Becky come meantime?'

Carefully suppressing her irritation, Alice said, 'She really wouldn't be much use in that short time. If I know Carol, once she has my OK she'll get moving very quickly. Besides, Becky would be more of a hindrance than a help at first.'

James nodded reluctantly. 'I see your point. I just thought it would be a kindness to Becky. Never mind, I'll tell her.'

'Now you've made me feel guilty but you must see that I can't take any risks. It isn't as if Becky has any experience of a veterinary nurse's duties. She might make some ghastly mistake. So you see—'

She stopped as he put up his hand. 'OK, OK, no need to get so defensive. I understand perfectly. The practice must come first in everything.'

'Well, under the circumstances, yes.' Alice looked at her watch. 'You seem to be having a quiet day—why don't you take the rest of the day off? As long as I know where I can get you in case of an emergency.'

'Good idea. My brother has some papers he wants me to examine so that's where I'll be.' James picked up his case. 'I'll tell Becky that you don't want her. She'll be disappointed, of course.'

Alice stood deep in thought as the door closed behind him. He seemed more concerned about Becky than was necessary. Perhaps he was falling in love with her. That would account for his protective attitude. Shrugging away a feeling of unease she went to tell her mother the good news in Carol's letter.

'Oh, that's marvellous!' Mrs Norton shared Alice's delight. 'Things are indeed looking up, aren't they?' She looked pensive for a moment. 'Why not let her live with us while she is looking for a flat? We get on well and there's plenty of room here.'

'Good idea. Let's ring her now.' Alice picked up the letter and searched for the number. Carol's voice on the other end of the phone sounded depressed but she reacted joyfully to Alice's suggestion.

'That will solve the last of my problems as this house is already sold. Quicker than I thought and the new people want to move in at once.' A few more words of conversation and then Alice replaced the telephone.

'She'll be here next week. What a piece of luck.' She paused and looked at her watch. 'Surgery in half an hour.'

'That reminds me—' Mrs Norton picked up the

message pad '—that case with the dog hit by a car. Front leg useless. The owner rang when you were out to say he'll be coming in this evening. He wants to discuss amputating the limb.'

'But it only happened recently. I told him it had a fifty-fifty chance.'

Her mother shrugged. 'The poor man can't bear the sight of the dog dragging her leg along.'

'Oh, dear. If it were my dog I'd wait at least because it might very well recover.' She sighed. 'Well, there it is. I suppose I'll have to do it. I think I'd like to have James's opinion. I'll ask him to join in the discussion.'

Mrs Norton said thoughtfully, 'I'd like him to assist you in the operation as well. I can stand most things but removing a limb from an otherwise healthy dog is a bit too much for me.'

Alice nodded understandingly. 'I'll ring him now. I know where he is.'

She rang him from her office and after he had agreed to her request she sat deep in thought. There was no doubt that she was beginning to depend on him more and more. He was so reliable and so helpful in every way but it was not only in a professional capacity that he appealed to her.

Reluctantly she confessed to herself that she found him very attractive as a man. Mentally and physically. He was good-looking of course but that was not the most important thing about him. There was something else—some kind of electricity she felt whenever she met his eyes and the way in which her heart leapt when he came into a room.

Was it just propinquity? Working together, sharing problems, united in their mutual love for animals? After all, she had led a rather narrow life for the last year or two, what with concern over her father's health and then the worry of taking on the practice alone. There had been no time for other interests.

Before that, there had been Edward. She could smile now at the intensity of her hidden grief when he had got engaged. How naïve she had been. That feeling which she had mistaken for love had certainly been due to propinquity so perhaps the same thing was happening again. She shook her head slowly. The last thing she wanted to do was to fall into another black hole like that.

As for James—well, while seemingly uninterested in women, he nevertheless appeared very protective of Becky and she was obviously besotted by him so she, Alice, must not make the same mistake she had made over Edward.

Ten minutes before surgery was due to begin James came into the office. 'Thought we should have a word together before this impatient man arrives.' He looked at her questioningly. 'Will you do the amputation if he insists?'

'I don't know. I really don't.' Alice paused. 'What would you do in my place?'

'I think I'd tell him to get another opinion— anything to delay the operation. When is he coming in?'

'He's bringing the dog with him at the end of surgery.' James frowned, hesitated a moment then asked, 'How are you on amputations?'

She shrugged. 'I've no fears on that score. After all, it's not all that difficult. But I might well refuse to do it if he insists.'

He looked doubtful. 'You'll lose a client. Are you prepared to do that?'

Alice sighed. 'I suppose I ought to look at it like that but—' She shrugged again.

'I know just how you feel,' he nodded sympathetically. 'Maybe the two of us can persuade him to give the dog more time.'

The sincerity in his voice made her say impulsively, 'I can't tell you how comforting it is to be able to share a problem like this with a colleague. That's where I found it so hard after my father's death.'

He said nothing but meeting his eyes she felt a slight shock. They were so full of tenderness that her colour rose. She looked away quickly and got to her feet. He did the same and said quietly, 'You're a brave girl. So long as I am here I'll help you as much as I can.'

She turned and met that same expression in his eyes again. As his last words sank in she said gratefully, 'You've helped me already. I haven't lost a single farmer, thanks to you.'

Suddenly he put his arm round her shoulders. Realising that it was only a friendly gesture, she smiled up at him. Then, gently releasing herself, she moved away, glad that he hadn't noticed the effect that his touch had had on her. A strange, unnerving effect—a kind of longing to be held tightly in those strong arms. She pulled herself together and said calmly, 'I can hear cars arriving. It is surgery time.'

There were not many cars and, because of heavy rain, not a lot of patients and Alice was glad that the waiting-room was empty when Mr Sanders walked in with Bess dragging along in a way that made Alice's heart sink. Lifted on to the table, the bitch was quiet and docile during examination, even wagging her tail as Alice stroked her.

She said, 'Well, there's no improvement but it's too early to expect any. She isn't in any pain and seems to accept her handicap as animals do in cases like this. There's nothing else wrong with her.' She paused and added pleadingly, 'I really think she should be given the chance of complete recovery.'

Mr Sanders shook his head sorrowfully. 'It's only a chance, isn't it? And not a very good one. I simply can't bear seeing her like this, knowing it was all my fault.'

He went on, 'And if, in the end, the slight chance doesn't come off then I shall have gone through months of misery for nothing. You say her general health is good. That means she can stand the operation, doesn't it?'

Alice nodded, then said, 'I could try large doses of Vitamin B, though I'm not sure that—' She paused. 'What about trying that for a month?'

'No,' Mr Sanders said determinedly. 'I've made up my mind. When will you do the operation? As soon as possible, I hope.'

Suddenly James said, 'It might be a good idea

to get a second opinion. We could find someone
independent for you to consult.'

Mr Sanders shook his head. 'I can't see any
point in that. Any treatment would still mean
months of waiting.' He looked at Alice. 'So will
you fix an appointment, please?'

Recognising defeat, she said, 'Tomorrow, if
that suits you.'

Once he had agreed, she gave him the necessary
instructions and when the door closed behind him
she looked at James and shrugged unhappily.
'That's that, then. Either I do it or someone
else will.'

'Don't look so distressed. It's not the end of
the world. I'll arrange my calls so that I can assist
you with the op. That's if you'd like me to.'

She gave him a grateful smile and nodded.
'You're quite right. I mustn't take it too much to
heart. After all, that patient of my father's is still
going strong after three years.' She gazed at him
thoughtfully. 'Do you think that being a man
makes it easier in cases like this? Are men harder,
less emotional?'

His eyebrows rose. 'That's a strange question.
I don't much like the idea behind it. Are you
implying that men have no finer feelings?'

'No—no—of course not.' She flushed, then
frowned. 'Well, perhaps I am. Look at the world
today—practically all the violence, the struggle
for power, wars have been caused by men.'

'Good Lord!' He stared at her mockingly. 'An
ardent feminist!'

'Well, that's just a label, isn't it? I don't call

myself that—I'm certainly not an extremist. But
I believe that women have got to stand up for
themselves. We've been kept down for thousands
of years.'

'Oh, dear! Oh, dear!' he said drily. 'I suppose
I ought to apologise for being a man but I'm not
going to.' He looked at her searchingly. 'Don't
you like men at all? Or have you perhaps had a
bad experience which has made you bitter?'

She flushed. 'I'm not bitter. Actually, I haven't
had much experience with men. I did imagine
myself let down once but that was my own fault.
I took too much for granted.' She stopped herself.
She was giving too much away. Hastily she turned
the conversation. 'You, on the other hand, have
certainly had a bad experience—your mother and
your fiancée killed—you have reason to be bitter.'

His face hardened. 'Who told you this?' Then,
before she could answer, he answered himself.
'Ah—my sister-in-law, of course.'

Guiltily Alice remembered that she had been
bound to secrecy and was immediately penitent.
'I'm sorry,' she said, 'I ought not to have
mentioned it.'

He shrugged. 'I expect you heard the wrong
version but I prefer not to discuss it.' He looked
at his watch. 'Don't forget your pregnancy
diagnoses.'

'Oh, goodness!' She picked up her case. 'I think
I can just about make it. Thank you for
reminding me.'

Alice's thoughts, as she drove along, were rueful. She should never have got into that silly

argument with James. Her stringent views on men had led to her breaking his sister-in-law's confidence.

But what was it he had said? She frowned as she remembered. That she had probably heard the wrong version—that was puzzling but she mustn't dwell on it. It was nothing to do with her. Concentrating on the task that lay ahead, she pulled up in the farmyard.

Mr Shelley was obviously pleased to see her and, as they walked towards the cowshed, he spoke of a new method of diagnosing pregnancies. 'I don't like the idea much because it's done by lay people but of course—' he grinned ruefully '—it's much cheaper.'

'You mean ultrasound scanning?'

He nodded. 'Yes. It's taken off in a big way around here but I'm not so sure of it when it comes to pregnancy diagnosis. We were talking about it at the last farmers' meeting. Fred Barker over at Underhill Farm was very strong about it. He had tried it out with one of the self-styled experts. Better than calling in an expensive vet, he said. Then it turned out later that one of his cows which he passed as pregnant wasn't. He had failed to diagnose a tumour.'

Entering the cowshed and pulling on her overall, Alice said, 'That's just the trouble. Untrained people doing the work of professionals. They are unable to recognise or understand the presence of anything abnormal.

'The veterinary college argues that scanning by rectal probe is an act of veterinary surgery and should be regulated under the Veterinary Surgeons Act and that lay persons offering the service should be advised that they must cease such activities.'

Mr Shelley nodded approval. 'You know your stuff, young lady. That's half the trouble nowadays. Technology is very wonderful and all that but when it gets into the wrong hands it can be very dangerous.' He paused and indicated the row of cows awaiting her 'Well, there you are. I'll abide by your verdict.'

It was not a pleasant job but Alice worked her way steadily through the sometimes indignant cows and finally announced, 'You're lucky this time. They're all in calf.'

'Ah, now that's what I call good news.' Mr Shelley pointed to a pail of water up against the wall. 'You can get most of the muck off your arm in that. Then you must come into the house and have a good clean-up and a cup of tea with my wife. She's always pleased to see you.'

Driving back, Alice felt a glow of satisfaction. Mr Shelley had told her that two more old clients of her father wanted her to do their work but understood that if she couldn't always get to them in time they would be content with James. That was just what she wanted.

Then a warning note sounded in her mind. She must make sure that when he came to the end of his engagement she must be ready with another male to take over.

Unless of course the question of a partnership came up again. Once more she turned the idea over in her mind and remembered that he seemed to have abandoned the scheme but that might be changed. She must endeavour to be practical and keep an open mind on the subject.

CHAPTER FOUR

NEXT morning James came in while Alice was preparing for the amputation operation and soon everything was ready and waiting for Mr Sanders's arrival. Having received his formal consent, she took charge of the sad-looking Labrador and waited for him to leave. To her surprise he shook his head.

'I'm going to sit in the waiting-room. Do you mind?'

'I really think it would be better if you went home. The operation may take some time. I promise to ring you as soon as it's over.'

Suddenly he seemed to go to pieces. Tears stood in his eyes as he gazed down at his dog. At last, looking up, he met Alice's compassionate expression. Drawing a long breath he said, 'I know you think I ought to wait longer and see if the fifty-fifty chance of recovery comes up.' He swallowed hard.

'I assure you I would prefer to do just that but I can't. My wife is an invalid and requires a lot of attention. The sight of Bess dragging her leg along is upsetting her so much that I have no option. I just hope that this operation will enable Bess to get around the house and accompany us when I push my wife's wheelchair out.'

'I'm sorry I misjudged you,' Alice said penitently. 'Of course you're doing the right thing and I'll do my best to enable Bess to live an active life.' After a moment she said, 'Why not go home and reassure your wife? She's not alone, is she?'

'No. Her sister is with her. Unfortunately, she—my sister-in-law—is the pessimistic type.' He came to a decision. 'I think you're right. I'll go back and try to be optimistic.'

Watching him leave, Alice said, 'Poor man. He's torn between his love for his wife and concern for his dog.'

James nodded. 'He's got his priorities right. His wife must come first.' He paused and added reflectively, 'Strange, isn't it, how life seems to hit people when they are already down? They say that troubles never come singly.'

'Oh, come on,' Alice said bracingly. 'They also say that you never get more than you can bear. When things get to breaking-point then nearly always something happens to lift the burden.'

'That hasn't been my experience.' His voice was bitter. 'Perhaps I haven't reached breaking-point yet.'

Yearning to comfort him, she said, 'Well, how's this for an example of what I mean? In my case, I was getting desperate about the practice and, at what seemed the last moment, you came along to solve my problem.'

His eyebrows rose. 'Good grief! Is that how you look on me? Sent by Fate to save the situation?'

She flushed. 'How else?'

'So it seems that there is some point in my existence, after all,' he said drily. 'What I would like to know is do I get any reward for rescuing you?' Suddenly he reached out and pulled her towards him. Holding her close, he said, 'What about this?' Bending his head, he kissed her. A gentle kiss that called for an equally gentle response.

She was so startled, however, that instinctively she tried to pull away and he immediately let her go.

Quickly she turned aside in case he should see that he stirred her in a way that she had never before experienced. Drawing a long breath to steady herself, she turned again and saw that he was standing as though in a trance. At last he said slowly, 'I made a mistake there. I'm sorry. I only meant to be friendly but—' He stopped, glanced at his watch and said coolly, 'Better get down to this operation, hadn't we?'

As soon as the anaesthetic had taken effect she began the grisly task which she accomplished calmly and efficiently, while James watched over the anaesthetic machine. Then, with the wound dressed and the necessary injections given, she breathed a long sigh of relief as together they installed Bess in a warm recovery cage.

'She'll need watching closely,' James said and Alice nodded. 'I'll stay here with her until she's fully conscious.'

'Would you like Becky to help you? No,' he contradicted himself sharply. 'I can see you wouldn't and I'm sure you're right. She wouldn't be any use in an emergency.'

Irritated by the way in which he seemed to be

so concerned over Becky, Alice said, 'Why don't you tell her to try another veterinary practice if she really wants to become a VN?'

He shrugged and picked up his case, pausing at the door.

'By the way, have you got a date fixed for going to dinner at your friend's house?'

'Not yet.' She looked at him curiously. 'Why do you ask?'

'Well, I want to fix an evening off. For a similar do.'

Alice said coolly, 'It doesn't matter to me. Just tell me which day you prefer.'

He nodded. 'I'll let you know when I've decided when and where. I shan't get back till rather late so please contact me if you have any night calls.'

She smiled. 'Don't worry. I can cope.'

'I know that. But I don't want you going out alone at night to a hitherto unknown client.'

She laughed a little scornfully, 'I wouldn't do anything so stupid. You needn't be so—well—protective.'

James gave her a steady look. 'A beautiful girl like you needs protection.'

She flushed but managed another laugh. 'That's very old-fashioned.'

'I am old-fashioned where women are concerned,' he said. 'Well, I'll take tomorrow evening off, then. That OK?'

When he had gone Alice found herself wondering who he was taking out to dinner but told herself firmly that it had nothing to do with her. Half an hour later, after telephoning Mr Sanders to put his mind at rest as much as possible, she gave her attention to the Labrador. Suddenly the door opened and, to her dismay, Becky appeared.

'I thought you would be here. I'd like to have a little talk with you. Can you spare me a few minutes?' Becky's smile was purposefully friendly and Alice's heart sank.

She said stiffly, 'I think I know what you want to discuss. Anyway, come into my office.'

Becky put her case very well and Alice knew that if it had not been for the imminent arrival of Carol she would be hard-pressed to refuse her request. She tried to be sympathetic and added, 'I thought I'd already made the matter clear to James. Didn't he tell you that our ex-veterinary nurse is coming back?'

'Oh, yes. He tells me everything, you know—' there was a hint of malice in Becky's voice '—but even then, couldn't I come in half-time to help out? I don't mind what I do and I don't want to be paid. I would just like to get a little experience, however elementary.'

In the face of such persistence it was impossible to turn down the request. Resentfully Alice said that she would consult with Carol and let Becky know later. Furious with herself for not being more desisive, she took some time to calm down before going back to her supervision of the Labrador. Then once more the door opened and she stared incredulously as Edward walked in.

He laughed. 'No, I haven't got a patient for you. May I come in?'

She shrugged. 'Well, you are in, aren't you? What can I do for you?'

He followed her into the office and sat down opposite her. Meeting his eyes, she recognised an expression she knew of old. An expression that, in the past, had led her to think that he cared for her. He had been the cause of much unhappiness but now she felt nothing for him. Coolly indifferent, she waited for him to speak and at last he broke the silence.

'You heard, of course, that Peggy and I broke up soon after we got to America?'

'Well, I only learnt that the other day. Why?'

'I'd like to know what effect it had on you.'

Alice stared at him. 'What an extraordinary question! It had no effect on me at all except perhaps a little mild surprise.'

He looked rueful. 'I suppose I deserve that. But I realised my mistake very early on. My mother tried to make me see that I had made the wrong choice. She told me that I should have noticed that you were in love with me but I was too infatuated with Peggy to listen to her.'

'Infatuation in my case too,' Alice said. 'Still, it soon passed off. I've grown up since then. A lot has happened in the two years that you've been away.'

She saw him wince and thought wryly how the roles were reversed. Now it seemed that he was the suppliant—at least, that was how it appeared—and his next words bore that out.

'Alice—I've learnt my lesson. I've come home

to see if you still loved me and to ask if you would marry me.'

'Good heavens! You're not serious—you can't be!'

He reached out across the desk and took her hand. 'Listen, I've got lots to offer you. I'm financially very prosperous and from now on I shall be based in England. No need for you to slave away any more. All I need is your forgiveness for being so blind.'

Alice tried to withdraw her hand but he held on tightly and she could only sit and stare at him. This man was so different from the rather boyish friend she had yearned over. Undeniably he was attractive—he had broadened out and and even his voice seemed deeper than she remembered. To marry him would solve all her problems but— She shook her head and opened her mouth.

Before she could speak, however, he went on urgently, 'I know what you're going to say— you're a vet and you want to go on practising. Well, I wouldn't stand in your way but you wouldn't have to work the way you are doing now. You would be able to afford to employ staff to take on all the heavy work and only do the cases you were interested in.'

He was quiet for a moment. 'I can see from your expression that I'm going too fast but promise me that you will think it over. Please.'

This time he let go of her hand but he still sat there looking at her so pleadingly that she knew she must be kind when giving her decision. For, of course, it could only be no. She didn't love him and never would.

Edward stood up and was about to say something when the telephone saved the situation for her. Thankfully she picked it up and listened carefully. James's voice brought her back to reality.

'I'm at Underhill Farm. A calving. Not an ordinary one—twins—very reluctant to come out. I'll be some time yet. Would you like to come along and join me? I might need your help.'

Her interest aroused, Alice promised to get there as soon as possible. She turned to Edward and explained that she was going out.

'How about letting me come with you? Just for the drive,' he added hastily. 'I'd stay in the car so I wouldn't be in the way. In any case that kind of case isn't my cup of tea, as you well know.'

She laughed. 'Yes, I remember how squeamish you were when I used to drag you into the surgery when my father was operating.'

He looked pleased. 'Well, there you are. Memories—we have those in common. I remember other things—' He stopped as she glanced at her watch.

'I must catch my mother before she goes out.'

'It's all right,' Mrs Norton said amiably. 'I've decided to stay home after all.' She paused. 'I saw Edward go into the surgery. Tell him he needn't go away. Tell him to come and have coffee with me. I'd like to see him again. Memories of old times.'

Gladly Alice passed on the message and Edward shrugged reluctantly. 'I suppose I must

go. As she says, it will be like old times when
you and I haunted each other's homes.'

It was easy to put him out of her mind and her
spirits lifted at the prospect of working with
James. Mr Barker, the farmer, greeted her as she
parked her car in the yard.

'I'm just going into the house for a minute—
I'll be back soon.' He paused and added gloomily,
'I just hope we'll get those twins out alive though
whether they'll be any good is a moot point.'

For a moment Alice looked puzzled, then her
face cleared.

'Of course—you don't want one male and one
female because then the female would be sterile.'

He nodded, 'That's right. Two heifers would
be best. Still, there it is.' He walked away and
Alice reflected that the farmer was concerned only
with money, whereas James would count any live
calf as a reward for all his work. And hard work
it was as she soon saw when she entered the
cowshed.

James was rubbing his right arm and said ruefully, 'It's a bit bruised. She's contracting so
fiercely that's she's almost paralysed my arm. I
must stop these contractions for a while so that I
can turn this first calf. Once I can get it into
position the rest should be comparatively easy. I
think the second one is still alive.'

Alice nodded. 'Shall I get the injection ready?'

'If you would,' he said gratefully and as soon
as she handed him the filled syringe he plunged
it in and stood back. 'It won't take long to work.'

Half an hour later James was looking very tired but Mr Barker was jubilant.

'Two little heifers—that's made my day.' He looked at the new mother. 'Is she all right? She's had a rough time.'

James nodded. 'Just as soon as her two little daughters start to feed. But we must keep an eye on her. I'll look in tomorrow.' He patted the cow. 'You've done a fine job, old girl.'

As they got into their respective cars James came up to her just as she was about to drive off. 'Let's call in at a pub. You must be hungry. I know I am.'

She hesitated. 'My mother will have something waiting. I don't think—'

'Oh, come on. Give her a ring. You deserve a break after a heavy morning. That amputation—'

'Oh, goodness! My mother said she would watch over it but when Edward came in—'

'Edward?' James frowned. 'What did he want?'

'Oh, nothing much,' but, remembering his unexpected proposal, she flushed vividly and saw James's frown deepen. Hurriedly she said, 'Yes. I'll ring my mother. May I borrow your mobile phone?'

Mrs Norton calmed her fears. 'The Labrador is coming round nicely. Edward has been keeping me company while I watched over her. He's changed, hasn't he? Improved, I think.'

'Is he still there?' Vaguely irritated by her mother's enthusiasm and forgetful of James's presence, she added, 'If he is, tell him I shan't be back for some time. James and I are having a pub lunch on the way back.'

'Oh, dear!' Mrs Norton said ruefully. 'I've asked him to share our lunch. Can't you skip the pub?'

'I suppose I'll have to. I wish you hadn't asked him.'

Handing the telephone back to James, she made a little grimace. 'Sorry about that. My mother—'

'I heard,' he said coolly. 'Your Edward must come first.'

'My Edward? He's not *my* Edward—just an old friend. But my mother always liked him and I rather think—'

He interrupted again, 'She wants you to get together once more. That's obvious.'

She shrugged and looked at her watch. Taking this as a hint, he said coldly, 'Well, enjoy your lunch,' and went back to his car.

On her way back Alice passed a pretty little pub and sighed. It would have been pleasant to have accepted James's invitation and it was annoying that her mother had unwittingly made her refuse it.

A feeling of depression swept over her. It seemed as though her life was being invaded by intruders leaving her no time in which to be herself. For a few more minutes she gave way to self-pity, then hastily she pulled herself together. Suddenly she realised that a lot of her troubles were of her own making.

Offered help and friendship, she was so determined to do everything herself that she was becoming hard and self-centred. Smiling ruefully to herself she turned into the drive of her home, parked her car and walked into the house.

It was then that she heard the sound of her mother's laughter and, filled with remorse, she realised that, since her father's death, it was a sound that she very rarely heard and once more guilt swept over her.

Bracing herself, she entered the kitchen and greeted her mother and Edward cheerfully. Mrs Norton said quickly, 'Don't think I'm neglecting your amputation case. I've only just left her— she's doing well.'

'I shouldn't have left you for so long. It's not fair that you should be so tied down by my work.' Alice bent down and kissed her mother lightly. 'I heard you laughing as I came in. What's the joke?'

'Edward has been amusing me by recalling the mad things you, Molly and he used to get up to.' Mrs Norton went on, 'I'm so glad you three have renewed your old friendship. Now that you've got James to help you should be able to get out more and with Carol coming next week life may get brighter for you.'

'For you, too,' Alice said quietly and there was a small silence broken at last by Edward.

'I'll gladly do my bit. For a start let's fix an evening out together.'

Alice hesitated. 'Don't rush me. Let's wait till Carol has settled in. She'll be here on Sunday evening.' Changing the subject, she said, 'I'd like to go and look at my patient.'

'Ten minutes to lunch,' her mother said as Alice got up and Edward followed her to the door.

'May I come too? Not that I care for ghastly sights much.'

'It's not ghastly at all. I flatter myself that I've done a very neat job.'

He grimaced. 'If that had been my dog I'd have had it put to sleep.'

She looked at him curiously. 'I don't believe you. It's easy to say that about another person's companion animal but when it happens to you, you feel quite differently.'

He laughed. 'On the principle that other people's children are little monsters, whereas your own are little angels.' He paused, and as they entered the recovery room he added softly, 'However, I'm sure that if you have any children they really will be little angels. Of course, if I have the luck to be their father—' He stopped as Alice turned to stare at him.

'You to be their father? Good grief, Edward— whatever gave you that idea?'

Unabashed he grinned back and shrugged. 'A man can dream, can't he? Two years ago you might have liked the idea, mightn't you?'

'Oh, yes,' she nodded thoughtfully. 'But I'm very glad now that I've grown out of what was only an illusion.'

'Is that what you call it?' Edward looked defeated and, for a moment, Alice felt sorry for him. But it had to be said and however much he persisted she knew that she mustn't surrender to his charm.

He waited while she attended to the bitch and a few minutes later they sat down to lunch. Edward seemed to have recovered his spirits and once more the talk became nostalgic. Then, as they were drinking coffee, the telephone interrupted the conversation and, to her surprise, Alice found herself talking to Becky.

'David has asked me to ring. He wants James to come and see to a sow who farrowed last night. She's had six piglets but she seems indifferent to them and won't let them feed.'

Alice said calmly, 'James is out but I can contact him. I'm sure he'll be over as soon as he can.'

She was tapping out a number when Edward asked, 'Why don't you go as you're available and he's not?'

'Because that's the arrangement. James does the large animals in order to keep the farmers happy. Apart from a few exceptions they are against women vets.'

'Well, so should I be if I were a farmer.' Edward shrugged. 'Maybe I'm old-fashioned but I think it's a man's job.'

'What nonsense,' Alice said mockingly, and as a voice came over the telephone she said, 'Oh, James—a call from your brother,' and gave him the message.

'Sorry—I shan't be able to make it for at least a couple of hours,' he replied. 'I'm working on a horse with bad colic. How are you fixed? Do you think you could manage it?'

'Of course.' Alice was pleased. 'I'll go right away.'

Explaining the situation to Edward, she was taken aback when he said, 'I'm at a loose end. May I come with you? I promise not to distract you.'

She shrugged. Why couldn't he accompany her? She must really stop erecting barriers between herself and the rest of the world. She smiled. 'Of course. It's not a very complicated case. Just a matter of giving an injection.'

He laughed as he followed her out to her car. 'What a strange life you lead. "Just a matter of injecting a sow"—most of the girls I have known would hardly know a sow from a boar and as for injecting one—' He grinned as he seated himself beside her and she laughed in return as she started the car.

'Well, you obviously haven't met any women vets,' she said. 'I expect all your girlfriends have been sophisticated types.' Suddenly curious, she asked casually, 'Have you had lots of girlfriends in America?'

'I've played around a bit but somehow—well, that's all in the past. The present is all I'm interested in and the future depends on you.'

'Now you are distracting me. I'm a vet, remember, and I don't want this sort of talk when I'm working.'

'Sorry,' he said penitently. 'I'll keep it till you're off duty, though as far as I can see you never are.'

'Vets have to give a twenty-four-hour service and in a small practice that can be difficult,' she said coldly.

'Almost impossible, I should imagine. I can't

think why—' He stopped and shrugged.

She took him up quickly. 'You can't think why I do it. Well I love the work—it's really a vocation like any career in medicine—and now that I have James to help me it's made my life much easier.'

Edward said nothing and, casting him a quick glance, Alice saw by his face that he was sulking. Suddenly she remembered that this was one of his characterics. Memories came back of times in the past when his plans were about to be frustrated and the way in which she and his sister had given in to him in order to keep the peace.

Of course, she told herself, nobody was perfect but sulkiness was something she disliked intensely.

Pulling up outside the house, she reached to the back seat and took out her case. Turning to Edward, she said, 'The pigs are round the back. Would you prefer to wait here?'

'Oh, I was hoping to see how you will deal with your patient.' Edward had recovered his good humour. 'I'm trying to get used to the weird things you have to do.'

She hesitated, nodded and as they walked round the corner of the house an upper window was flung open and Sophie called, 'David had to go into town but Becky is with the pigs. I'll come as soon as I can.'

Alice frowned. She could do without Becky, who wouldn't be best pleased either to see her. Sure enough, Becky's welcoming smile faded as they approached. She said brusquely, 'Why hasn't James come?'

Alice controlled her spurt of anger and explained the situation and Becky said, 'Well, I suppose you'll do. That's if you can do the job.' Then, staring at Edward, she said sarcastically, 'Or have you brought another vet with you to help?'

Once more Alice bit back a sharp retort and managed a cool smile as she introduced Edward. Turning towards the range of pigsties she asked, 'Which is the sow in need of the injection?'

'Over there—the last but one,' Becky shrugged. 'You'll never be able to do it on your own. She's not a very nice character. Apt to turn on you as soon as you approach her with a syringe. It would have been better if James had come.'

Pointedly ignoring them both, Alice studied her patient. The sow was lying on her stomach so that the piglets couldn't get at her and after a few moments' thought she bent down, opened her case and took out a syringe which she filled with the requisite dose of pituitrin. The sow raised her head as Alice went into the sty but before she could react the needle was plunged into the thin skin lying behind the ear.

'Phew!' Edward wiped his forehead as Alice quickly shut the sty gate behind her and asked, 'Why on earth did you inject behind the ear?'

'Because that's the only place on a pig where a fine needle can be used,' she said calmly as she put the syringe back into her case.

As she stood up, Becky said coldly, 'I think you took an unnecessary risk. It doesn't pay to take a chance with a newly farrowed sow. I should have thought you would have known that.'

Now was the moment Alice wanted. This scornful, know-all girl must be put down and she proceeded to do just that.

'Experience—and I've had plenty—has taught me just how far one can go with pigs. I could hardly leave that sow without attention and make her wait for an indefinite period until James turned up.' She paused. 'You stick to your job, Becky, and I'll stick to mine.'

'Well said.' The deep voice behind her startled Alice for a moment and she turned to see James grinning approvingly. 'I managed to get here sooner than I thought but I see you've beaten me to it.'

'Oh, James!' Suddenly Becky was all sweetness and light. 'Do you think the sow will be all right? After all, large animals are your speciality, aren't they?'

Alice held her breath in anger and even Edward was staring at Becky in surprise but James laughed and pointed towards the pigsty. 'Well, look at the miracle Alice has worked.'

All eyes turned to look at the sow and the piglets who were pushing and falling over each other to get at the milk which was already flowing copiously.

Forced to acknowledge that all was now well, Becky shrugged and said, 'Well, I must go back to the house.' Ignoring Alice, she smiled at James. 'See you later.'

CHAPTER FIVE

As ALICE walked towards her car she saw that Becky had turned back and was talking to James. For a moment she felt a twinge of—what was it? she wondered uneasily—jealousy? Oh, no! She frowned in self-rebuke. Certainly not that. She must get things in proportion. James was not her exclusive property.

Deep in thought, Edward's voice brought her to reality. 'You're very preoccupied. Are you brooding over that girl's obvious antagonism towards you?'

'Antagonism? Well—' she hesitated '—I think that's just her manner. All the same—' she shrugged '—I must admit that she doesn't seem to like me much.'

'And the feeling is reciprocated, isn't it?' he said drily. 'I wonder why. Personally I get the impression that for her part she looks upon you as a kind of rival.'

Settling herself into the car, Alice turned sharply. 'What on earth do you mean?'

'You know very well what I mean. She feels about you as I begin to feel about James.'

She stared at him and he gazed back at with a hint of mockery in his answering smile. At last she said coldly, 'You're letting your imagination run away with you. There is no such thing as rivalry between Becky and me. Nor should there be between you and James.'

'Well, we'll leave Becky out of it but I can't help feeling a bit uneasy about you and James. That there's something between you, I'm sure.'

'The only thing that links us is our work,' Alice said sharply. 'For goodness' sake, stop imagining things. What's more, you mustn't keep on insinuating that you know me better than I do myself. You don't. I've changed a lot since the days when—'

'The days when I got engaged to Peggy? You were clever at disguising your feelings then, weren't you? At least that's what my mother has told me. I actually had no idea at the time.'

'Well, of course not. You were utterly obsessed with Peggy.'

He took her up quickly. 'And if I had never met her and had asked you to marry me, would you have said yes?'

She flushed. 'Probably. And have lived to regret it because what I felt for you then was not real love. Thank goodness you went away.'

'That's a bit cruel.' He looked downcast and for a moment she felt sorry for him but she knew that she must be cruel in order to be free of him. She added firmly, 'Let's change the subject. I find this one very boring.'

He subsided into silence and when she pulled up outside her garage she said a little more kindly, 'I'm not going to ask you in. I've got a lot of work to do.'

He seemed to revive and her heart sank as

he said, 'We still haven't fixed a date for dinner together. Come on, Alice, I'm an old friend. Don't brush me off entirely.'

There was genuine feeling in his voice and she weakened reluctantly. The prospect of an evening out was tempting but she didn't want to be alone with him. She said, 'How about Molly? After all, she was my particular friend in the old days.'

'What?' He frowned. 'Oh, don't be silly. She wouldn't want to play gooseberry.'

She shrugged. 'No Molly, no dinner.'

He got out of the car and stared down at her. 'Is that your ultimatum?'

She nodded, smiling inwardly, and walked towards the house. A few moments later he called after her, 'All right. I'll ask her tonight and we'll fix an evening. Sure you don't want our mother as well?'

The sarcasm of Edward's last words made her laugh, Then she dismissed him from her mind as she greeted her mother.

Mrs Norton said, 'I've just been cleaning up the Labrador. She's standing up—a bit wobbly of course—but she getting stronger all the time. By the way, James is here—he tells me he thinks Mr Sanders is fetching her this evening. Isn't that a bit soon?'

Alice shrugged. 'I'm inclined to think it is. I'll just go and have a look at her.'

James looked up as she entered the recovery room. 'She's marvellous—see how she is beginning to get her balance. Another day or two and she'll be mobile. Don't you think it might be better to keep her here until then?'

Alice frowned. 'Well, I'd prefer to but Mr Sanders might want her back. Shall we wait and see how he reacts when he sees her? After all, she's not exactly a pretty sight at the moment. And she'll want watching carefully.'

But Mr Sanders took the sight of his pathetic Bess very well. He nodded as Alice explained that she would look much better once the stitches were out and the hair had grown over the wound.

'Of course,' she added, 'it all looks very conspicuous now with the bandages on but once they're off she'll adjust very quickly to her handicap.' She paused for a moment. 'Wouldn't you like her to stay here another day or two?'

He shook his head. 'I've prepared my wife— told her she would be shocked at first—and she's accepted that. I think she needs Bess and Bess will be so happy to be home that it will probably help her recovery. Do you think she can walk to the car?'

Alice shook her head. 'That's a bit too soon. Once she's in her own bed at home she must be left to find out for herself just what she can do. Now, let's fix an appointment for me to see her. I'll come to your home and examine her.'

That having been done James said, 'If you'll bring your car right up to the door I'll carry her.'

Once safely installed in the hatchback, Bess already looked happier. 'She even wagged her tail as she recognised familiar surroundings,' said James on his return.

As he looked at Alice he said quietly, 'Don't

cry. I know you're sorry for that poor man but you can be proud of a good job well done.'

She flushed at his praise and wiped her eyes. 'I'm sorry for the poor dog, too.'

'I know,' he said sympathetically, 'but you deserve pity as well. Pity for the hard time you've had since your father's death and the way you're struggling to keep the practice going, along with all the hard work and long hours it involves.'

Tears threatened Alice once more but she blinked them back and smiled mistily. 'Things will be easier when Carol arrives,' she said. 'It will make a great difference and now that you've come my workload has been halved.' She paused. 'It was the greatest piece of luck when you rang up that first evening and agreed to help me out.'

'Not luck,' he said quietly. 'You said Fate. I think we—' He stopped abruptly then said, 'Time for surgery and judging from the sounds in the waiting-room it's going to be a busy one. Would you like me to help?'

Alice nodded gratefully and soon they were working their way through a variety of patients. Dogs and cats predominated, mostly with routine problems—fleas, mites in ears, worms and digestive troubles caused by faulty diets. Given tablets, ointments and necessary antibiotics, the patients came and left in quick succession.

There was also the inevitable sadness of having to put a much loved pet to sleep. It was always more traumatic for the owner than for the old and tired dog or cat. It was a task that Alice hated and she was only too thankful when this evening

James quietly took over and gave the necessary injection.

One or two dental cases she put off to the following week, knowing that Carol could do the professional scaling very competently.

A pet rabbit with a large abscess on its face had to be lanced and the resulting smell left Alice feeling mildly sick. Given an injection of antibiotic it was handed back to its owner and as she turned away Alice saw that James was looking at her concernedly.

Before calling in the next client he came over to her. 'Look—go and sit down in the office. I'll finish out here. You look dead tired.' In spite of the fact that she shook her head, he led her firmly through the door and sat her down at her desk. Suddenly picking up her right hand he said, 'What's this angry-looking scratch on your wrist? A cat?'

She nodded. 'A rather fierce cat. It's nothing.'

'Nonsense! Let me see to it.' Bending over her, he smeared on an antibiotic ointment and as he smoothed on a dressing Alice suddenly felt an almost uncontrollable urge to stroke his thick dark hair.

'There.' He finished his task and looked up. 'Now, I'll see to the remaining patients.' He laughed gently. 'You're free for the rest of the evening and so go indoors, have a nice restful bath and I'll take you out to dinner.'

She smiled but shook her head. 'I can't possibly. My mother is cooking a meal. Besides—'

'I know all the objections but they can easily

be dealt with.' He picked up the telephone and spoke to Mrs Norton. He grinned as he rang off. 'Your mother thinks it's a very good idea. She'll put through any really urgent calls so let's see— an hour should give you plenty of time.'

'No; thank you but it's still no.'

He stared. 'For heaven's sake—why not?'

'Well,' she said slowly, 'first of all I'm not going to treat my mother as a willing slave. She's been tied to the phone far too much lately and secondly I just don't like being pushed around.'

James frowned. 'That's a bit unkind.' He studied her intently. 'It boils down to one thing. It's me, isn't it? I bet if it was Edward asking you, you would go like a shot.'

Startled, she said sharply, 'That's ridiculous! I don't want to go out with anyone this evening.' She got up and went towards the door. 'Leave it like that, please, James.'

Suddenly Alice felt herself being pulled back and as his arms enfolded her heart began to beat wildly. The look on his face rendered her speechless and she gasped as he bent to kiss her. Then, just before their lips met, he drew back and let her go. For a few moments she stood very still, half-afraid to walk away in case her legs let her down.

As though in a dream she heard him say, 'I'm sorry! I'm sorry! Please forgive me.' He swallowed hard. 'There's something about you that—what I really mean is—' He stopped, then shook his head. 'All I know is that I want to help you, protect you—'

His voice deepened as he added quietly, 'Old-fashioned words but the only ones to describe the way I feel about you. There is, of course, one word that emcompasses all those feelings but—' and in a voice that was suddenly harsh, he said, 'Forget what I—' He shook his head. 'I can't give you an explanation. Please try and understand.'

Alice was so bewildered that she began to grow angry. She said sharply, 'How can I possibly understand when you give no explanation?'

He said nothing and she lost patience. 'Look— it doesn't matter. Your mysterious hints are exasperating and I rather think that they are just excuses to get you out of an embarrassing situation.'

'No!' He spoke so sharply that she fell back a step. 'You mustn't think that. You've got it all wrong.'

'Got what all wrong?'

'You wouldn't understand.' He turned away. 'Just forget everything, please.'

She watched him go and shrugged her shoulders resignedly. There was obviously some reason for his strange behaviour but if he didn't want to divulge it there was nothing she could do other than try to forget the effect he had on her.

Unfortunately, it was not easy. That night she slept badly as her imagination took over. It was not only the questions to which she could find no solutions that troubled her. It was her fear that she might be falling in love with a man who seemed to find her attractive but who had some strong reason for not letting his feelings get the better of him.

Was he beginning to fall in love with her? Was it too much to hope that one day she would learn the secret that held him back from—she frowned—back from what? Was he ever going to confide in her or was it, as she had accused him, just a ploy to get out of difficult situations? That would be despicable. She could hardly bear to contemplate it and yet the possibility had to be faced.

Resolving to keep a guard on her own feelings for him, she drifted into a troubled sleep.

Next day the Saturday morning surgery was busy. James came in for a few minutes before going out on calls. He was his normal self, joking with Mrs Norton who was helping Alice and congratulating her on the way in which she managed to calm nervous patients. She laughed ruefully. 'When Carol comes on Monday I shan't be needed here any more.'

He smiled. 'I'm sure you'll always be needed. Mothers are the one stabilising influence in this unsettled world.'

There was a small silence after he had gone and then Mrs Norton said thoughtfully, 'There's something rather sad about that young man. That bit about mothers—his mother was killed as well as his fiancée in that awful accident. I expect he was thinking about that.'

Alice, on the point of opening the waiting-room door, stopped in her tracks. That might well be linked up with James's strange behaviour. In that case there was nothing she could do about it. After all, she only knew what his sister-in-law had told her and that, according to James, was inaccurate.

Puzzled, she went on attending to her patients while telling herself that when an opportunity presented itself she would try to find out more from Sophie. Even if, as James had said, she was wrong it might be possible to learn something that would put her on the right track.

Some of the cases that morning were a little awkward in that the owners were so vague in their descriptions of their pets' symptoms that Alice had to give up listening to them and diagnose without any guidance whatsoever.

Her mother, who was helping, appreciated her difficulties and said thoughtfully, 'Doctors certainly have it easier to find out what's wrong with their patients. Ours can only look at us pathetically while their owners often mislead us with talk of trivialities.'

Alice nodded resignedly and went to wash her hands while Mrs Norton made coffee but just as they were about to sit down the bell in the reception area rang sharply. A minute later Alice found herself face to face with Becky.

In answer to Alice's question, the other girl smiled. 'I can see I'm too late—your surgery is obviously over. But I only want some worming tablets for my dog and as I was passing I thought I'd drop in and pick them up.'

It seemed a lame excuse but Alice nodded. 'I'll

want some details first. You know—weight and other relevant information.'

While giving the necessary details Becky's eyes were everywhere. At last she asked casually, 'Is James anywhere around? I'd like a word with him.'

'Out on calls,' Alice said briefly and as she counted out the worming tablets she added, 'can I give him a message?'

'Oh, no, thank you,' Becky answered then said, 'Well, yes, perhaps you can. You may see him before I do. It's just to say that I may be a little late this evening—about half an hour.' She smiled in friendly fashion but there was malice in her cold eyes. 'He's taking me out to dinner this evening. All rather sudden but he takes decisions quickly, doesn't he?'

Alice shrugged indifferently and handing her the tablets said, 'The directions are on the leaflet inside.'

'Thanks. Oh, dear—' Becky looked in her bag. 'I'm afraid I haven't got any money with me. I'll have to give it to James this evening.' She nodded goodbye and then turned at the door. 'I'm off to get myself something nice to wear tonight.'

Mrs Norton laughed caustically. 'If she's got no money with her she'll find it difficult to shop.'

Alice shrugged. 'She can always pay by cheque.'

'She could have done that here. Oh, I know you don't charge for worming tablets as a rule—it's such a small amount and clients are to be encouraged to worm their animals regularly.'

Mrs Norton looked thoughtful. 'She was very

anxious that you should know that James was taking her out. Do you think there's anything going on between them?'

As Alice was thinking along the same lines she found it difficult to appear indifferent but, as casually as she could, she dismissed the subject. For the rest of the day she concentrated on her work and it was not until James appeared at the end of evening surgery that she remembered Becky's visit. When she mentioned the worming tablets he looked puzzled.

'There was no need for her to come here for them. I gave her some the other day.' He frowned. 'I'm sorry she didn't pay. Anyway, here's the money. Can't have the practice penalised.'

She smiled and glanced at her watch. 'Hadn't you better be going? Becky said you were going out to dinner.'

'Good Lord, I'd almost forgotten. You can get me if necessary at the Swan Hotel. That's a place I'd like to take you—perhaps you could find an evening next week. You need to get out sometimes.' He grinned. ' "All work and no play makes Jack a dull boy," you know.'

'Well, thanks very much,' said Alice resentfully. 'In that case I expect you'd find me a very boring guest. I'm sure you'll find Becky much more interesting.'

'Becky—what's she got to do with it?'

Alice was saved from replying by the sound of the telephone and signalling goodbye to James she picked up the receiver. It was a request for information but she managed to prolong the conversation until she saw James glance at his watch and, seemingly reluctant, he left.

Then she gave herself up to indignant thoughts. The idea that she would want to be taken out to dinner at the very same place he was taking Becky tonight—it was almost humiliating.

Calming down, she smiled wryly. It was obvious that he was playing a deep game. It wasn't a pleasing thought but she must give him the benefit of the doubt and hope that one day he would confide in her. Unless of course Becky—there her heart sank and she had to put the depressing thought aside.

Later that evening Edward rang. In accordance with her wishes he said that Molly had agreed to join them for dinner and how about fixing a date? What about this very evening?

'No, I can't—not this evening. James is going out and I'd rather stay at home in case of emergencies. Also, my mother is going to visit a friend.'

There was a moment's silence before he said, 'So you'll be on your own?'

'Yes. Let's put it off till next week when Carol will be here.'

She could see in her imagination the sulky look on Edward's face but to her surprise he agreed amiably and rang off. She looked down at the telephone thoughtfully. Edward had certainly improved. The prospect of an evening out with him seemed more attractive, especially as Molly would be there.

Evening surgery was not busy and eventually

Alice settled down to a solitary meal. It was rather pleasant to be on her own and she hoped fervently that the telephone would remain silent. Thankfully it did and, engrossed in listening to music, she almost missed the sound of the doorbell. But at last she heard the persistent ringing and getting up reluctantly she went to the door and found Edward smiling at her.

She said nothing for a moment then with a shrug she ushered him into the sitting room and turned off the music.

'You look unusually relaxed.' He settled himself in an armchair and she sighed inwardly. Gone was the quiet evening that she was enjoying so much.

She said, 'I was until you arrived.'

He laughed. 'Nice welcome. Actually I came on impulse. It occurred to me that with no one around I might at last have the chance of an uninterrupted talk with you.'

She said coolly, 'I'll get some coffee.'

'If you don't mind, I'd rather get down to what I want to say.' He looked at her meaningly. 'Surely I'm too old a friend to be treated formally. Listen, Alice—I want to get things straight. I've admitted that I made a mistake with Peggy. I'm going to ask you again. Will you marry me?'

'Oh, dear!' Alice gave a heartfelt sigh. 'I'm sorry, Edward, but it's still no. You must accept that. Nothing will make me change my mind.'

Edward's face darkened. 'Can't you ever forgive me for going off with Peggy?'

She shook her head despairingly. 'It's nothing

to do with that. You must believe me when I tell you that I don't love you—never did really. You're just nostalgic for the past.'

'It's not the past I'm interested in—it's the future.' He frowned. 'I suppose you think you're in love with this James fellow. Well, you'll be unlucky there. He's the "love 'em and leave 'em kind" from what I've seen.'

'That's not true,' she said vehemently, then realised suddenly that she had no grounds for that statement. Seeing the mocking smile that greeted her outburst, she forced herself to speak lightly. 'Well, you might be right for all I know but what I meant was that it's not true that I'm in love with him any more than I am with you.'

She stopped and congratulated herself on having got out of a tricky situation. She added smoothly, 'Now let's drop the whole subject and talk of something else.'

'There's nothing else to talk about,' he said sulkily, 'I'd better go.'

He got up slowly just as the telephone rang but sat down again as she picked it up. She listened intently and said, 'You'd better bring her in now and I'll do what's necessary.' Replacing the telephone, she stood for a few moments deep in thought. At last she turned to Edward. 'I've got to stitch up a dog. She's torn herself jumping over barbed wire. I really need someone to help me.'

Edward looked uneasy. 'Where's James?'

'Out,' she said briefly, 'and so is my mother, as you know. It's only a question of helping me to give a light anaesthetic which I do by injecting it into a vein. I can do the rest alone. I just want you to hold the dog while I, with your help, get the vein up.'

He forced a smile. 'I'm not sure I can even do that. There'll be an open wound and I'm allergic to the sight of blood.'

Alice stared at him incredulously. 'I'm not asking you to look at the wound—I don't suppose there'll be much blood anyway.'

'All the same—' he edged towards the door '—I think you'd better call James back. Sorry and all that but there it is.' He added, 'I'll go and fetch him if that will help.'

'Don't bother,' Alice said very coldly. 'I've no doubt the owner will help.'

But there she was wrong. Mrs Court was indignant when Alice asked her. She had far too much to do—packing, and so on—she was going on holiday soon. She would come back for Timmy early next morning in order to get him into kennels. 'I'll give you the address,' she added, 'then you can go over and take the stitches out later on.'

Alice nodded and continued her search for the gash in the little dog's thigh. At last she looked up. 'I thought you said it was a huge gash. The only thing I can find is this small tear—it only wants a local anaesthetic and one stitch.'

'Well, it looked bad enough to me. Anyway I still prefer to leave her with you.' She looked around disapprovingly. 'I must say I would have expected to see a few more people around. Are you sure you can deal with Timmy on your own? I'd no idea this was such a small practice. I rather wish—still, it's too late now—' She shrugged disdainfully and departed, leaving Alice tense with anger.

This gradually changed to depression as she worked on her patient. While she waited for the local anaesthetic to take effect she stood thinking about Edward. A broken reed if ever there was one. But her depression went deeper.

The simple fact was that she could not run this practice on her own with only occasional help. Of course, Carol would be here next week but, even then, facts must be faced. But not now because this little dog must be dealt with.

The local anaesthetic had taken effect but her patient, being fully conscious, was getting nervous and restless. She must find a way of getting it under control. Frowning for a moment, she quickly changed her expression and spoke soothingly but with little effect and she hesitated with the threaded needle in her hand.

Suddenly, to her great relief, the door opened and Mrs Norton walked in. Taking in the situation at a glance, she held the dog firmly while Alice put in a stitch and tied it off. Snipping the thread, she smiled her thanks and carried off her rebellious patient to the recovery room.

Mrs Norton laughed. 'That was lucky. Mavis had a headache and I thought it better to leave early. Tell me—why didn't you call one of us back to help you?'

Alice hesitated. 'Well, it was such a small thing and I thought Edward would help me but—' She shrugged ruefully.

'Edward—he was here?'

'Yes. Oh, it's a silly story. He came to see me and was just leaving when this case came up. He was utterly useless. Let's forget it and have a cup of tea, or something. I've got a problem and I'd like your advice. James made me an offer some time ago which would save this practice and bring it completely up to date but it would mean giving him a partnership. It was a very generous offer.'

Alice went on to give all the details and waited for her mother's reaction. It was slow in coming but at last Mrs Norton asked quietly, 'So why did you turn it down?'

Alice shrugged. 'You know very well that my big ambition is to build up Dad's practice to what it was and to do it on my own.'

Mrs Norton nodded. 'Yes, I know that but I also know that your father's plans were to take in a partner—you, of course—then later on another partner, who would put money in to buy his share and eventually take on an assistant. I know this because he told me himself. The day of the solo vet is over. You have to expand or close down.'

She sighed and looked at Alice compassionately. 'You must face facts, my dear.' She was silent for a few moments then she said firmly, 'James has come up with a wonderful offer. I think you should accept it.'

Alice frowned. 'It would mean that I lose control. James will want so many changes.'

Mrs Norton looked round the surgery. 'Changes are necessary. Technology can't be ignored.'

Alice nodded reluctantly. 'But it's James—I'm not sure that I know him well enough. He's rather—well—mysterious.'

'Mysterious? That's absurd! I think he's still suffering from the effect of that dreadful accident in Australia. His fiancée and his mother—' She shook her head. 'That was bad enough but to have his father marry again so soon afterwards—that must have hit him hard.'

Alice hesitated. 'But there's another thing. I think—well—I feel almost sure that he's very interested in Becky. He might even marry her, then I'd have her to contend with as my partner's wife. I'd hate that.'

'Becky? Is that the girl who works for his brother? Do you dislike her?'

Alice nodded. 'There's a kind of animosity—we seem to rub sparks off each other.'

'Hmm, don't you think you're imagining things?

'No, I'm not. Actually he's taken her out to dinner this evening. He's obviously keen on her.' Aware that her mother was looking at her sceptically, Alice gave up. She said, 'The point is: shall I reopen the subject about a partnership?'

'Why not? It's a very handsome offer. And it comes from a man I consider to be utterly trustworthy even if you don't.' She laughed gently and went on, 'Well, that's my advice but it's entirely up to you. I shan't reproach you if you decide against it.'

'Well—' Alice pondered for a while '—this is what I'll do. James has several months to go

before his time here is up. Anything could happen
before then so I'll wait for a while before broach-
ing the subject again.'

CHAPTER SIX

CAROL arrived at lunchtime on Sunday and while they enjoyed a celebration meal she said, 'It's so kind of you to let me bring Sammy with me.' The little Norfolk terrier looked up at the sound of his name and Mrs Norton stroked him wistfully.

She said thoughtfully, 'You know, I miss having a dog. Our old springer spaniel died soon after my husband—just pined away in spite of all we did to try and console him.' She paused and looked at her daughter. 'What do you think, Alice? Shall we fill the gap that Jason left?'

Alice nodded enthusiastically and the talk revolved around the new idea. Gazing reflectively at Carol, Alice felt a great sense of relief. Somehow, having this sensible, warmhearted friend back gave her a feeling of security and confidence.

The two of them working together would show clients that the practice was still strong and Carol's advice on future developments would be invaluable. Her thoughts were interrupted by her mother.

'You tell Carol about James while I make coffee,' she said and as she went towards the door she added, 'I've already told her how desperate we were getting before he answered your advertisement.'

'Well there really isn't much to say.' Alice

hesitated for a few moments then gradually found herself opening up and praising him warmly. The fact that she was intrigued by his mysterious behaviour she managed to keep to herself. It was when she told of his generous offer and the doubts she felt about it that she saw the puzzlement on Carol's face.

She finished abruptly just as her mother came in with the coffee and after a thoughtful silence Carol said, 'Well, I don't know all the ins and outs, of course, but at first sight it seems the answer to all your problems. So why on earth did you turn it down?' She turned to Mrs Norton. 'Do you know?'

Alice's mother shrugged. 'I think I do. She finds it difficult to let a comparative stranger have equal rights in the practice.' She paused and added loyally, 'You must admit it's a difficult decision.'

Carol nodded slowly. 'All the same—'

She stopped as Alice said quickly, 'Equal rights at first but it wouldn't be long before he took over in a big way. He has already said, "we need that, we need this, and that"—all things that are very expensive and it would be his money that would pay for the big changes he thinks are necessary.'

'Well, that's the point of putting money into a practice. Nowadays if you don't progress then you will gradually go downhill.'

Alice saw her mother nod in agreement and suddenly she felt isolated. How could they understand? They only saw the practical side. But emotionally—that was so involved that she dreaded committing herself to something that she might come to regret.

Her face must have betrayed her doubts for Carol said, 'I think I understand how you feel, Alice, but one day you'll have to take in a partner. You can't settle for a succession of assistants who will come and go and are so difficult to get. Especially when they realise that there won't be any future for them in the practice.'

Alice nodded. Carol had put the problem into a nutshell and grateful as she was for such unbiased advice she felt as if the ground had been cut from under her feet.

Seeing her daughter's evident distress, Mrs Norton said briskly, 'Well, there's still plenty of time yet to decide.' She turned to Carol. 'It will be interesting to know what you think of James when you meet him.'

They met the following morning just before surgery and it was soon evident that they would get on well together. Carol nodded approvingly as he went away but said nothing until after surgery was finished.

It had been reasonably busy and it was plain that Carol had lost none of her own skill. With her expert help, patients were soothed and calmed while Alice was able to concentrate on diagnosis and treatment. She felt as though her workload was halved and said so when at last they sat down to coffee.

Carol said, 'Well, now that I've met James I'm absolutely sure that you'll never find another vet more suited to this practice. Don't turn down his offer, Alice. You won't get another like it.' She paused. 'You say you refused him—was it quite definite?'

'It was mutual. In the end he withdrew his offer but I haven't seen any signs of him looking for another job. Of course he may be going to put up his plate somewhere.'

Carol sipped her coffee thoughtfully and said, 'How do you feel about him personally? I mean as a man—not as a vet?'

Alice felt her colour rise but she said evenly, 'That's difficult to answer. I quite like him but—' She stopped as she met Carol's quizzical gaze and shook her head.

'Honestly, I don't know. Sometimes I like him too much for my own comfort but at others I even resent him being here. I'm afraid—' She paused, then with a great yearning to confide in her old friend, she added slowly, 'I'm afraid of facing up to the truth. I know subconsciously that I'm on the verge of falling in love with him and it's making me very uneasy.'

'Why? Are you afraid of being rejected? Or is there someone else he's interested in?'

'I don't know, or rather—well—there's Becky. He seems to be rather keen on her.'

'Becky who? Tell me more.'

Alice finished her coffee and then with a shrug she answered her friend's compassionate curiosity. She ended by saying, 'I just don't like her and it's obvious she doesn't like me.'

There was silence between them for a few minutes before Carol said slowly, 'And yet she wants to work here and James is trying to get you to agree to take her on. Well, why not? Let her come and I'll take her in hand and at the same time I'll find out which way the wind blows between her and James.'

She laughed. 'When she's found out the unpleasant work that is entailed she may not be so keen on becoming James's helpmate and I mean "mate" if that's her little game.'

Alice looked doubtful but was unable to voice her objections as the telephone interrupted their conversation.

The caller was very agitated. 'It was all so quick. The lorry came round the corner and Judy—my corgi—was just coming across the road. I don't think the driver even saw her—he went tearing on—and Judy was flung into the gutter. I carried her into the house but she's unconscious. Please come at once.'

Taking the name and address, Alice turned to Carol. 'I expect I'll have to bring her back here. Will you set up everything? You know—blood transfusion, possible operation.' She picked up her case and checked. 'Everything is there. I'll be off.'

Half an hour later she returned and shook her head in answer to Carol's enquiry. 'The dog died just before I arrived. I tried a heart stimulant but it was no good. The owner made me furious. She said Judy was turned out every day and only came in for meals. That way she had plenty of exercise and didn't mess up her immaculate house. People like that make me livid.

'Into the bargain, they had a garden but, like the house, it was excessively neat and tidy and the dog was never allowed to play there. Her husband, she said, would bury Judy at the far end and that would save the cost of having it disposed of in the usual way.' Alice put down her case and added, 'I was so furious that I felt like charging her double for calling me out.'

'Did she pay?' James's voice sounded amused and, turning quickly, Alice saw him standing in the doorway.

'No,' she said briefly. 'She said she hadn't any cash in the house and didn't have a bank account.'

James grinned. 'No wonder you're furious. Still, it suits you. You look like an avenging angel.'

Carol chuckled but Alice, suddenly self-conscious, said, 'I suppose I am going over the top a bit. Sorry.'

'Don't apologise,' James laughed. 'Nice to know you have a tender heart. I was beginning to wonder.' Ignoring Alice's indignant gasp, he added, 'Changing the subject—have you told Carol about Becky? Working here part-time, I mean.'

How persistent he was, Alice thought irritably, but tried not to show her displeasure as she turned to Carol. 'You said you wouldn't mind, didn't you?'

Carol nodded and smiled. 'She can take over some of the more unpleasant jobs so naturally I don't mind.'

James frowned. 'You're joking, I hope. "Dirty jobs"—that's not quite what she imagines.'

'Well, no. Carol isn't joking,' Alice said coolly. 'It's a good way to begin. It soon sorts out the sheep from the goats. You should have warned her.' She paused, then added smoothly, 'When you took her out to dinner the other night you could have prepared her.'

'Took her to dinner?' He looked bewildered, then his face cleared. 'Oh that wasn't possible. It was a family do with my brother and sister-in-law. It was Sophie who suggested Becky to make up a fourth. Did you imagine she was my only guest?'

Hardly able to disguise her pleasure, Alice said calmly, 'I didn't imagine anything. I just took Becky's words at their face value. She said, "James is taking me out to dinner." Anyway, it doesn't matter.'

She saw James's mouth tighten, knew that he was displeased and felt a little jubilant. Carol broke the uneasy silence by asking a few questions about Becky to which James replied briefly, then said, 'Alice will fill in all the rest.'

As he turned towards the door he said quietly, almost as though he were talking to himself, 'I've done my bit. Now Sophie can stop pestering me.'

Carol stared at Alice. 'That was very odd. What on earth did he mean?'

Alice shook her head. 'Haven't the faintest idea. I only hope we shan't repent our decision. I feel uneasy already.'

'No need to worry. I haven't met the girl yet but I think I can see her little game.'

As if I hadn't guessed already, Alice thought, but she merely asked, 'Can you really?'

Carol grinned. 'Come off it, Alice. You know perfectly well. She's out to catch James and her reason for wanting to work here is that she can keep an eye on what goes on between you and him.'

'Well, she'll be wasting her time, then.' Alice shrugged indifferently and changed the conversation. A few minutes later the telephone rang and Carol picked it up.

'My job from now on,' she smiled but a few seconds later she handed it over. 'James's sister-in-law. She wants you.'

After listening carefully, Alice said calmly, 'I'll come right over and help you.' Replacing the telephone, she turned to Carol. 'Sophie has found a stray dog in the barn. Obviously a stray—in very poor condition and very nervous. She wants to get it away before the children come back from school.'

Driving along, Alice found that she was unable to get Becky out of her mind. The thought of having someone she didn't like working with her in however humble a capacity was worrying. Annoying, too, because the pleasure of having Carol back was going to be diminished to a certain degree. All confidential talk would be banned and the atmosphere would, of necessity, be stiff.

She sighed heavily and pushed the problem aside as she pulled up outside the farm. Soon Sophie came running out to greet her and as they went towards the barn Alice heard the story.

'He ran in here as soon as he saw me and I haven't been able to lure him out. I put a bowl of water and some food just inside and shut the doors. I must get him out before the children come home. They always rush in there to look for any eggs the chickens may have laid among the hay bales.'

As they stood in front of the closed doors she lifted the wooden latch and peered in cautiously. 'He's still there and—yes—he's eaten the food.'

As they approached the dog backed away growling. Then, gradually responding to Sophie's soothing voice, he slowly wagged his tail while still shrinking back against a bale of hay. At last he took a few steps forward and crouched at their feet.

With a swift movement Sophie slipped a leather lead over his head and in spite of a frightened whimper he remained still. 'He's been badly treated,' Alice said. 'Look at that swollen eye. There are burns on his back as well, poor little thing. What will you do with him after I've treated him?'

Sophie glanced at her watch. 'The children won't be back for some time. Let's take him into the kitchen and give him some food.' She paused and sighed. 'Unfortunately I can't keep him. He needs careful nursing and I've got more than enough on my plate as it is. I suppose I ought to ring the police to see if anyone claims him.'

She paused. 'I'll bet he was attached to that band of so-called "Travellers" that invaded one of the fields down the lane. The police managed to evict them about ten days ago. The mess they left behind was awful and there were several dogs trailing around.'

Alice said, 'I'll take him back with me and treat that eye and the burns. Actually—' she looked pityingly down at the little creature, shivering with fear as they led him gently towards the house '—he has the makings of a pretty little thing. Partly West Highland terrier, I should think.'

In the kitchen Sophie opened a tin of dog food and put it on the floor. After a short hesitation the dog began to eat. In a minute the bowl was empty. Suddenly he seemed a different animal. No longer trembling, he looked up at the two girls, wagged his tail and began to scratch vigorously.

'Oh, dear!' Sophie laughed. 'Well, it will be up to you to get rid of those fleas. But before you go I'll make some tea.'

A few minutes later, the dog peacefully asleep, Alice listened as Sophie described her daily routine. 'Not that I'm highly organised,' she said ruefully. 'I do the most urgent things first and try to ignore any job that can be put off for a while.

'A woman asked me the other day if I didn't yearn for a proper job and hinted broadly that I must get terribly bored without the stimulus of work outside the home.

'When I told her that I got all the excitement I needed with a large old house, a husband and children to care for, to say nothing of the animals and emergencies that seem to crop up every day, she looked at me so scornfully that I began to feel I was a bit abnormal.'

Alice laughed, helped herself to a biscuit and said thoughtfully, 'And now you have the addition of your brother-in-law. More work than ever.'

'Oh, James is no trouble. He and David get on so well, although their characters are totally different. Mind you, James has changed a lot since that terrible accident. He won't talk about it, you know.'

Remembering James's statement that his sister-in-law had 'got it all wrong', Alice asked cautiously, 'Which death affected him the most? His fiancée's or that of his mother?'

Sophie frowned. 'Well, I've never really considered that question. Perhaps that of his mother. His relations with his fiancée always seemed unsettled. They used to fight quite a lot—she was very demanding, I believe. He seemed to worship the ground she walked on but there were rumours about her—

'Poor James. Still, he ought not to brood on it the way he seems to. David and I would like him to get married to some nice girl and forget the past.' She brightened up suddenly. 'I hear that Becky is hoping to work part-time in your surgery. Is it arranged or don't you want her?'

Alice hesitated. 'Yes, although actually I'm not too keen myself but Carol—my veterinary nurse who has come back to us—says she will show her the ropes.' She paused. 'James has been very persistent.'

'That's good.' Sophie looked pleased. 'I'm rather hoping that they'll get together.'

Suddenly Alice didn't want to hear any more.

Glancing down at the sleeping dog, she said, 'Must get back. I'd like to get him cleaned up before surgery. Thank you for the tea.'

The little stray was very reluctant to leave Sophie's kitchen but eventually he settled down in Alice's car with an air of resignation that she found both sad and touching.

He was equally submissive when he was being cleaned up and treated for his injuries. At last, standing back to admire the result of their handiwork, Alice said to Carol,

'Apart from that bruise over his eye which will soon go he'll be perfectly fit in a few days. I'm pretty sure the police will be only too glad to leave him with us. Though I really don't know—'

She stopped as Mrs Norton came in and began to pet the dog. Glancing at Carol, who was smiling and nodding, she saw that the problem was solved.

Gathering up the little dog after listening to its history, Mrs Norton said, 'Just what I needed. I'll give him a lovely life.'

There was a lump in Alice's throat as she saw the dog reach up to lick his new mistress. Mrs Norton spoke softly to him, then looked up. 'I'll call him Angel—' she smiled tremulously '—sent to comfort me.'

It was so moving that Alice could hardly restrain her tears. Then Carol said laughingly, 'I don't suppose Angel will be house-trained so I expect he'll be called something else from time to time.'

Mrs Norton smiled. 'I'm sure he'll soon learn

civilised ways,' she said, and, putting Angel down, she went to the door. The little dog hesitated, then, as his new mistress called gently, he looked at Alice and Carol for a moment. Mrs Norton called again and suddenly he rushed to her and was gathered up again into her arms.

It took a little while for Alice to recover her composure then she said half-laughingly, 'You must think I'm over-sentimental but I'm so glad to be able to give something to my mother after all she's been through.'

'I understand very well,' Carol said quietly and Alice remembered that her friend had nursed and finally lost her own mother. It made a bond between them and they talked quietly together until Carol looked up suddenly. Pointing to the window she exclaimed, 'Heavens! Look at that rain! We won't have many people in this evening.'

Only two clients came in, both requiring booster injections for their pets, and when they had gone Alice said, 'Why don't you go into the house? I'll follow in a few minutes—I'm just going to look out the vials for Angel. I don't suppose he's ever had an injection in his life so I'll do him when I come in.'

Going to the fridge, she selected the necessary preventative doses and was about to follow Carol when the door opened and James stood shaking his jacket in the passageway. He laughed ruefully.

'What a night! I guessed you wouldn't be busy so, having heard from Sophie about the stray, I thought I'd like to have a look at him. If he isn't claimed, I might—' He stopped as Alice shook her head and went on to explain the situation.

He nodded. 'That's the best thing for him. He needs a loving home and your mother needs something to comfort her.'

'You're very perceptive and you're right. My mother doesn't go around with a long face bewailing her fate but I know that she misses my father dreadfully. They were devoted to each other.'

There was a short silence while Alice thought sadly of the time when her parents had been together, then James said, 'Well, that little dog will do more for her than even you can do. He will give her life new purpose.'

The depth of feeling in his voice made Alice look at him with fresh eyes. His sympathy was almost more than she could bear and once more tears gathered in her eyes. She turned away but James pulled her back.

'What have I said? Why are you crying?' His voice was so troubled that she managed to blink back her tears.

'It's only the thought of my father and mother—I must pull myself together.'

'No,' he said softly, 'don't do that. Let yourself go. It will do you good.'

He drew her closer and the comfort in those strong arms was overwhelming. All the stress and strain of the last months seemed to disappear as she relaxed against him. It was as though she had found a refuge from all her troubles and as his grasp tightened she yielded herself up to him.

As she heard him murmuring words of comfort she suddenly felt ashamed of her emotional breakdown. She began reluctantly to draw back but he said softly, 'Don't be embarrassed. I only want to help you. Let me wipe those tears away.'

Taking out a large white handkerchief, James gently wiped her cheeks and as she looked up at him she saw such tenderness in his eyes that her heart seemed to stop beating.

Suddenly, he glanced over her shoulder and those eyes blazed with fury as he demanded harshly, 'What the hell are you two doing here?'

CHAPTER SEVEN

SHOCKED, Alice pulled herself out of James's arms and gasped with anger as she saw Becky and Edward standing in the doorway. She was speechless as she stared at them.

Edward said coldly, 'Well, well! What a pretty scene! I suppose we should apologise for breaking it up. We should never have walked in unannounced.'

Becky's eyes were full of fury as they passed from Alice to James and at last she said, 'I might have guessed. Sophie said you would be hard to pin down but Alice seemed to have succeeded where I've obviously failed.'

Alice drew in a quick breath but James, carefully replacing his handkerchief, said very quietly, 'You're talking nonsense. Now, will one of you please state your business, then go.'

'Oh, yes, we'll go. It's very evident that we're not wanted,' Edward said sarcastically. 'Actually, I wanted to fix a dinner date with Alice but now—' he shrugged '—no point in that.'

Becky, still staring at James, said, 'I merely came to see the stray dog. I thought I might give it a home. Instead, I caught you out, didn't I? Quite a revelation.' She turned to Alice. 'Obviously I shan't be coming to work here now. I see why you were so reluctant to have me.'

She stalked out of the room and Edward was about to follow her when he stopped. Facing James he said, 'I can't help thinking that I'm entitled to an explanation. How serious are you with regard to Alice?'

This was too much. 'Don't talk about me as though I'm not here,' she said. James began to speak but Alice went on angrily, 'There is no explanation due to you. In other words, you should mind your own business.'

For a moment Edward looked taken aback and, turning to James, he said spitefully, 'I suppose I should congratulate you on knowing a good thing when you see it. A ready-made veterinary practice with the beautiful owner thrown in. You'd have been a fool not to jump at the chance.'

'Why you—' James took a step forward but, with a quick glance at his furious face, Alice grasped his outstretched arm. He shook her off but the momentary distraction halted him and with a derisive laugh Edward shrugged and went out of the room.

With a huge sigh Alice relaxed, but tensed up again as James said slowly, 'I'm terribly sorry to have caused such trouble between you and Edward. Somehow I must make him see that he has misunderstood the situation. Try not to be too upset. I'll put things right between you.' He paused.

'Obviously he won't talk to me so I'll write a letter.' He went towards the office. 'Would you mind waiting? You can read what I've said.'

Stunned and chilled, Alice was glad to have a

few minutes alone in order to get her troubled thoughts sorted out. It was her reaction to James that was causing turmoil in her mind. She knew now that she loved him but the joy of that discovery had been destroyed by his apparent lack of any similar feeling towards her.

It was humiliating to think that he was writing to Edward to say, in effect, that she, Alice, meant nothing to him and that Edward was, so to speak, welcome to her. She frowned angrily and drew a deep breath. She was not going to be disposed of like that.

Opening the office door, she said, 'Don't write that letter, please, James.' She stopped as he looked up in astonishment, then went on firmly, 'I'd rather ignore the whole thing. I don't care what Edward thinks.'

James looked at her searchingly. 'You're taking rather a risk, aren't you? You don't want to lose him, do you?'

'Lose him? Oh, James, don't be so thick! Why don't you believe me?'

He shrugged. 'Well, I suppose I must. Personally I think you're just putting a brave face on it. All right—I take that back. No need to look so furious.

'All the same, if I were in Edward's shoes I should be pretty mad if I saw the girl I wanted in another man's arms. Then, on asking for an explanation, to be told to mind my own business—' He grinned. 'Damn funny when you think about it!'

Reluctantly Alice could feel laughter welling up

inside her. At last, unable to control the quivering of her lips, she said drily, 'Quite melodramatic!'

Suddenly they both collapsed into helpless laughter and for a few minutes Alice's spirits soared. A bond had been forged between them. A bond of friendship and a shared sense of humour—working together; surely that was the way to go forward. The fact that she was in love with him was beside the point. She could keep that hidden. It was better than losing him entirely.

Sobering down at last she said, 'James—about your suggestion of a partnership—I know I turned it down but I've changed my mind. I think we could work something out, don't you?'

To her surprise he said nothing for a few minutes and then she remembered how, angered by her reception of his offer, he had withdrawn it and said that he would leave, as first arranged, when his six months had expired. At last, to her relief, he nodded slowly. 'It's up to you. What does your mother think?'

Alice frowned. 'This is my own idea. I'm not being pressurised by my mother.'

He shrugged and shook his head. 'You misunderstand me. I mean that I wouldn't like to enter into any agreement with you that displeased her. After all, here I am a complete stranger being made a partner in something that she helped build up.' He paused. 'Before we settle anything definite I think we ought to find out how she feels about it.'

'Well, of course, if you feel like that you'd

better come and see her and find out if you are acceptable.'

James's eyebrows rose at the sarcasm in her voice. He grinned. 'I'm sorry. I'm being tactless, aren't I? I sound like an old-fashioned suitor insisting on getting your parents' permission to marry you. Still, they do say that a partnership is like marriage—one should be very cautious before signing on the dotted line.'

Alice felt her colour rise. Hastily she changed the subject. 'By the way—what should I do about Becky?'

'Becky?' he laughed shortly. 'I don't see why you should do anything.' He frowned. 'What was it she said to you? Something about you having succeeded where she had failed? What the hell did she mean?'

Alice's heart seemed to miss a beat but she said calmly, 'I can't imagine. You'd better ask her yourself.'

'Hmm.' His eyes looked at her searchingly for a few moments and then he said quietly, 'I wish I could read your mind. It would help me enormously.'

She said nothing but as they went into the house and settled down for a talk with her mother she promised herself to try and work out what he meant when she was alone. The business talk was very satisfactory and when, after a celebratory drink, James left, she and her mother continued to plan for the future.

At last, alone in her bedroom, she tried to puzzle out the meaning of his strange desire to read her mind. After discarding various possible explanations she gave up. It would be more to the point, she thought sadly, if she could sort out her own feelings towards him.

Drifting off to sleep, she felt a glow as she recalled the tender, gentle words with which he had comforted her. Even if he had only acted out of friendship it was still a memory that she would always cherish.

Next morning James joined Alice and Carol for their after-surgery coffee and the talk turned onto the treatment that Alice had just been giving to Angel, the little stray dog.

'He's getting on very well and is so happy with my mother,' Alice said. 'Thank goodness there's no sign of him being claimed by his former owner. It's always so sad when a stray is brought in and is sometimes so badly hurt that it has to be put to sleep. It's also sad if an owner loses a well-loved pet.'

'That's something that's been on my mind for some time,' James said thoughtfully, 'and I think it would be a good thing to go in for the identity chip scheme.'

Carol looked interested. 'I've heard about it, of course, but I'm a bit vague as to how it operates.' She turned to Alice. 'Do you know?'

'Well, I know it's a microchip which is implanted under the animal's skin. It gives full details of ownership. This is linked up with a register. When a scanner is passed over the animal, that information can be read and strays and stolen pets can be quickly traced.' Alice paused. 'There's more to it than that, of course,' she said. 'It's one of those things we'll have to go in for one day.'

'As soon as we're fully computerised,' James said firmly and the authority in his voice made Carol stare at him and then glance questioningly at Alice.

Mrs Norton took in the situation and said quickly, 'Come outside with me, Carol, and I'll put you in the picture.' As they went out of the room Alice heard her mother say, 'James and Alice are going into partnership and—'

As her voice died away, Alice said coldly, 'You're going a bit over the top, aren't you? Surely there's no need to splash out on every bit of technology at once?'

'Why not? Don't you want to have all the latest equipment in your surgery?'

'*My* surgery?'

He gazed at her steadily. 'I see what it is. You're afraid that I shall take over completely. That's right, isn't it?'

She hesitated then said quietly, 'Yes.'

He closed his eyes momentarily, as though in despair at her attitude. 'In that case we'd better put a clause in the partnership agreement that you have the power to veto anything I suggest.'

'That's ridiculous!' she said scornfully. 'That wouldn't be a full partnership.'

He sighed. 'I thought we'd settled all that yesterday evening. Perhaps it might be better if I were only the junior partner.' He paused then shook his head firmly. 'No—sorry, but I can't agree to that. Equality or nothing.'

There was a long silence, broken suddenly by the sound of the telephone. As Alice picked it up James said coldly, 'Think it over and let me know as soon as possible.'

She nodded and, handing him the receiver, she said, 'For you.' A minute later he picked up his case. 'I'll be at the Marshall Riding School—a horse gone lame. See you later.'

As soon as his car had driven off Carol appeared and with a quick glance at Alice's flushed face she said quietly, 'Your mother asks if you would go and have a word with her. She seems a bit upset. I'll look after things here.'

Mrs Norton was certainly tense and Alice sighed to herself at the prospect of another argument. It was bad enough having to fall out with James again but even worse to have to explain everything to her mother. Why couldn't she be left alone to fight her own battles? She was about to try and put this as tactfully as she could when Mrs Norton took the words out of her mouth.

'I can see from your face that you and James are at cross-purposes again. Now—I've decided that I don't want to be drawn into your constant rows. It's not that I don't sympathise with you— I do, and with James as well—but you and you alone must make the final decision.'

She paused and looked steadily at her daughter. 'There's only one thing I must say. If your father had had an offer like the one you are subconsciously fighting against he would have jumped at it. He wasn't a stick-in-the-mud, you know.'

Alice winced. Was that what she was—a stick-

in-the-mud? The idea hurt, especially when it
came from her gentle, easy-going mother, and,
unable to find a suitable answer, she smiled ruefully and returned to the surgery. Half an hour
later Edward rang and as Carol handed over the
receiver with a whispered, 'More trouble,' Alice
shrugged and signalled to Carol to stay and listen.

His voice was cold. 'I can't remember if we
agreed on a dinner date but if we did then I think
we'd better call it off, don't you? We obviously
have nothing in common any more and in view
of the scene Becky and I witnessed yesterday—'

He broke off and Alice said gently, 'No need to
be so melodramatic, Edward. Actually, you
jumped to the wrong conclusion but it doesn't
matter.'

'It mattered to me,' he said angrily. 'It mattered
to Becky, too. Poor girl! She told me that James
had completely let her down. She was so upset
that I decided to take her out to dinner instead
of you.'

'You do that, Edward.' Alice stifled a laugh.
'I think it's a very good idea. You can console
each other.'

There was an angry splutter as he slammed
down the receiver and Alice turned to meet
Carol's wide-eyed astonishment and began her
explanation.

She tried to make light of the way in which she
had broken down but was unable to cover up
James's method of comforting her. When it came
to the dramatic finale Carol burst out laughing.
'Oh, dear! It's just like a romantic film. You

know—hero and heroine caught in the act—'

'Carol! How can you?' Alice looked at her friend indignantly, '"Hero and heroine." Good grief! Nothing like that!' She turned away. 'Let's forget it.'

'Easier said than done,' Carol said unrepentantly. 'Still, it's got Becky off our backs. I wonder how James will like that.'

Alice shrugged indifferently. No one must guess her secret. Her love for James must be kept under cover and it shouldn't be too difficult in view of his obvious wish to keep their friendship completely platonic.

Suddenly there was the sound of a dog barking and the door was pushed open by a large German shepherd, pulling his owner into the room.

'Wants his nails cut,' the elderly lady announced breathlessly. 'I'll hand him over to you and wait outside. He'll be quieter if I'm not with him.' She looked doubtfully at the two girls. 'Can you two control him?'

'Don't worry.' Carol laughed. 'We have our ways of dealing with difficult patients. Nothing cruel, I assure you,' she added hastily, seeing the alarm on the client's face. Taking the lead she led the dog towards the table.

Surprisingly he was docile and obedient and the job was soon done. When Alice opened the waiting-room door she saw that his owner was deep in conversation with a girl who had obviously been regaled with tales of her difficult pet. Handing over the dog, Alice said, 'Quiet as a lamb,' and then laughed apologetically as the owner was nearly knocked down by the exuberent greeting she received.

Shaking her head, the client said, 'He's too much for me. I think I'll have to change him for a smaller dog. I got him to protect me but I'm the one who needs protection.'

A few words of advice came from Alice, to which she paid little attention, and then, as the dog pulled away, Carol shook her head. 'Some people will never learn,' and the waiting girl laughed.

'Lots of folk like that. I meet them all the time in Australia.'

Alice turned quickly and looked with interest at the newcomer. Very pretty, slim and suntanned with long chestnut-coloured hair, she smiled and said, 'I'd better introduce myself. Janey Spencer, veterinary surgeon from Perth, Western Australia. I work for Mr Preston and I'm looking for his son, James, who I understand is doing a locum here.'

Alice caught her breath, glanced quickly at Carol and saw that she too was taken aback. Pulling herself together, she said smilingly, 'Yes. James works here but he's out on a call at the moment.' She continued, 'Unless he knows you're coming here he's going to get a nice surprise.'

Janey laughed. 'I like surprising people. Now, what shall I do? Go and surprise his brother— I'm going to ask them to put me up—or may I wait here till he comes back?'

'Would you like me to contact him on his mobile phone?'

'Oh, no.' Janey paused. 'That is—well—will he be coming back here?'

Alice nodded. 'I shouldn't think he'll be long. He went to see a horse over at the local riding school.' She went over to the window. 'We'll see when his car comes in. In the meantime, meet Carol—our veterinary nurse.'

It was while they were talking that Alice heard the welcome sound of James's car and a few minutes later he walked in.

'Didn't take long,' he said. 'It was only— Good God! Janey—I don't believe it!' Going forward, he gave her a big hug. 'Tell me why you've come.' Suddenly he paled. 'Nothing wrong with my father, is there?'

'No, no, he's fine. I'm on holiday so I thought I'd bring you some news. Good news.'

Alice said quickly, 'You can talk privately in the office.' She opened the door and waved them in.

As it closed behind them, Carol said, 'Well, she surprised James, all right. I wonder what the good news is.'

Alice looked troubled. 'I just hope it doesn't mean that he will have to return to Australia.' She sighed. 'It would mean the end of all our plans.'

Carol nodded, then said hopefully, 'Things may not be as bad as that. Let's stay here till they come out. We may learn something then. Meanwhile, I've got the dispensary to sort out. We need some replacements.'

Twenty minutes later the office door opened and one glance at James's face was enough to tell Alice that he had suffered some kind of shock.

He was even paler than before and walked as though in a daze. Strangely enough, Janey was smiling, though there were traces of tears on her face.

She said calmly, 'We're going over to see David and Sophie now. We'll be there for the rest of the day so if James is wanted you'll know where he is. Bye for now.'

Suddenly James turned. 'I'll come in early tomorrow morning. See you then.'

When they had gone the two girls gazed at each other in silence for a few moments. Then Carol said, 'Goodness! Something's up, all right. Perhaps he'll tell you tomorrow—he said he'd be in early.'

Alice shrugged but she felt sick at heart. The thought of losing James was almost more than she could bear. Never to see him again—the possibility of that brought home to her the depth of her carefully suppressed love. It took precedence over everything—nothing else mattered. How she was to get through her work until tomorrow morning she hadn't the faintest idea.

Carol, with one look at her stricken face, took charge. 'It's time for lunch but I don't suppose you want to go into the house so I'll tell your mother you're very busy and ask her for a sandwich and bring it back here.'

Alice nodded gratefully and for the short time she was alone she managed to pull herself together. It was no use speculating—she must absorb herself in work and build up her strength enough to withstand any blow that she might have to face in the morning.

Evening surgery, to her great relief, was busy and a little more varied than usual. A parrot with a chill, due to having been left in a draughty passage, was prescribed antibiotics and a pet ferret with advanced cancer had to be put to sleep and its owner—a young boy—had to be consoled. This was a task that proved so difficult that it took a long time.

A pet duck was brought in with a bad gash on its back. The owner was a girl of twelve who, while they were waiting for the necessary local anaesthetic to take effect, said that she had a problem.

She was, she said, a farmer's daughter and she had taken on the baby duck when she found him abandoned by his mother. She had spent hours every day tending and feeding him until he was strong enough to fend for himself. Kept in the house, he followed her everywhere and obviously looked upon her as his mother.

'I call him Donald,' she said, 'but now my father says he ought to be put back in the pond with the other ducks. Well, I've tried but they attack him and then he comes straight back to the house looking for me.'

She stood calmly watching while Alice put in two stitches, then lifted him off the table and he settled in her arms like a baby while she stroked him lovingly.

Alice smiled. 'I think you'll have to keep him until he's big enough to hold his own against the others. In any case he must be kept quiet until I take the stitches out. It won't be long before he will leave you of his own accord but even when living on the pond I expect he'll always remember you so you'll be able to keep contact with him.'

When she had gone Carol said, 'Nice little girl. Sometimes I wish—' She stopped, then asked hesitatingly, 'Don't you have a subconscious longing for children? And a husband too, of course,' she added hastily and laughed for a moment at her rueful admission.

Alice turned away to hide the tears that were too near for comfort. Of course she wanted children but only if they had James for their father. Drawing a long breath, she thought she had hidden her feelings from Carol but the next moment she felt her friend's arm round her shoulders.

'Sorry—that was tactless of me.' Carol's voice was full of sympathy and, grateful for her friend's understanding, Alice said brokenly,

'I don't think I can bear it if he goes back to Australia.'

'Listen.' Carol shook her gently. 'I don't think he will. At least—' she hesitated '—not without you.'

Alice stood back and stared unbelievingly. 'Are you crazy? What on earth do you mean?'

'I mean that James is in love with you though he tries to hide it. Why, I don't know, but perhaps this news he has had will bring things to a head.' She stopped and smiled. 'Onlookers see most of the game, you know.'

Somehow Alice got through the rest of the day. No calls came through for James and she went to bed early with Carol's words echoing in her mind. It couldn't be true. He had admittedly said things which seemed at the time to have a hidden meaning but even when he had kissed her he had always apologised as though he regretted his action.

She tossed and turned restlessly as sleep eluded her and finally decided that her over-heated imagination was working overtime. Carol, too, was letting her romantic mind see signs that bore no resemblance to reality. Finally Alice drifted off into a troubled sleep and awoke next morning heavy-eyed and listless.

CHAPTER EIGHT

DETERMINED not to show her curiosity, Alice greeted James casually when he walked in while she and Carol were having coffee after morning surgery. To her surprise, he also was behaving as though nothing had happened.

'Called out before breakfast,' he said lightly. 'A difficult calving over at Valley Farm. Mr Thompson is one of your loyal farmers but he rang me because he suspected twin calves and he thought the job might be too much for you.'

Alice frowned. 'Oh, dear. That old story. I'm sure I could have coped.'

'I expect you could and I suggested he ring you but he said he didn't want you to lose any beauty sleep.'

'Stupid thing to say.' Alice slammed down her coffee. 'Why are these farmers so sexist?'

'Old prejudices die hard.' James laughed as he helped himself to sugar. 'By the way, he has a bull that needs an injection and wants me to do it. I agreed because I really think—'

'There you are—no better than the farmer,' Alice said crossly. 'I've often watched my father treating bulls—some of them massive creatures. There's nothing to giving an injection so long as there is adequate help.'

James looked uncomfortable. 'Well, I promised

I'd do it. It's for a bronchial condition and I have to be there at twelve noon.'

Alice said no more but when James had left to do more calls she turned to Carol. 'No ops this morning so I'm going over to Valley Farm. I'll have to get there early and I'll tell Mr Thompson that James has been held up so I've come instead.'

'Alice! That's crazy. You've never actually treated a bull yourself, have you?'

'There's a first time for everything and so long as the bull is under control it's no different from any other farm animal.'

'Maybe—but what about James? He won't like it much.'

Alice shrugged. 'Probably not, but I'm still the boss around here and Mr Thompson is one of my so-called loyal farmers.' She paused and added ruefully, 'Not as loyal as all that. He called James out to that calving this morning.'

Carol said, 'You'll have to resign yourself to the fact that where there's a man in the practice a farmer will always prefer to deal with him. After all, that's the reason you took James on, isn't it?'

'Oh, I know but—well—' Alice stopped. Carol was right, of course. She said lamely, 'It's probably because my so-called loyal farmer has deserted me that I want to show him up.'

'Hmm. I don't think that's the real reason.'

'What on earth do you mean?' Alice asked. Seeing the sceptical look on her friend's face she just shrugged and said no more. Glancing at her watch, she opened her case to make sure that she had the right antibiotic for injection and a large syringe capable of piercing the bull's tough hide. Satisfied with her preparations, she pulled on a jacket and called over her shoulder, 'You know where I'll be. Wish me luck.'

Carol shook her head disapprovingly. 'You worry me at times. Do take care.'

Mr Thompson consulted his watch with a puzzled air when Alice greeted him. 'Mr Preston isn't coming till twelve,' he said. 'You're a bit early if you've come to watch.'

Alice forced herself to smile. 'No. I've come to treat the bull. Mr Preston may not be able to get here on time.' She paused. 'I know I'm early but I have quite a lot of work waiting for me.'

'You? A slip of a girl dealing with my bull? You must know how savage he can get. Your father had a way with him but he'd had years of experience.'

Struggling to speak pleasantly in spite of her irritation, she said, 'May I see the bull—Angus, that's his name, isn't it?'

'Ah, you remember him.' Mr Thompson looked mildly pleased. 'All right. I was just going over to his box.' As they set off, he added, 'Can't think how he's got into this state. Off his food, breathing badly—fast, shallow breaths—and very bad-tempered.'

'Well, he'll need treating with antibiotics. First injection today.'

Mr Thompson stopped and stared at her for a moment but, seeing the determination in her face, he said slowly, 'Well, I don't know—' He called out, 'Jim—come over here, will you, and help

with the bull. He's got to have an injection.' Alice
greeted the herdsman cheerfully, recognising him
of old, and he grinned. 'Taking over from your
pa, are you? I'll just get the necessary.'

As they approached the box in which Angus
was housed they were greeted by a hoarse roar
as the massive animal struggled to his feet and
stood glaring at them. His eyes were red and
angry, showing a general hatred of the human
race who were keeping him a prisoner, but to
Alice he seemed pitiful and lonely and each of his
shallow breaths was obviously causing him pain.

The herdsman walked up to the box and deftly
inserted a stout pole in the ring in the animal's
nose. Turning to Alice he said with a grin, 'The
only way to control a brute like this. But mind
you get the injection in properly. You won't get
a second chance—he could break that door down
if he went beserk.'

Alice nodded and looking round she said, 'You
know this box won't be very helpful towards his
recovery. It's badly in need of repair. The wind
is whistling in through those holes in the wall
behind him. When I've given him his injection do
you think you could find a warmer box for him?'

Jim's tanned face grew slowly red and Mr
Thompson nodded. Obviously smarting over the
rebuke, he said gruffly, 'Just like your pa you are.
He was always on about giving the animals the
best of everything.'

'Well, it pays off in the end, doesn't it? Angus
here might not have had this bronchial trouble if
he'd been better protected against the bitter winds

we've had lately and then you wouldn't have my
bill to pay.'

She stopped as she saw her shaft had gone
home. Mr Thompson shook his head. 'Just like
your pa,' he repeated and then, recovering himself, he added, 'Well, let's see if you can get that
injection in as well as he used to. "Nothing to
it," he would say, "just a question of getting of
through that tough skin."'

Alice opened her case and took out a bottle of
antibiotic liquid. Very carefully she measured out
the required quantity into a large syringe and tried
to quell the nervousness caused by the critical
gaze of the two men.

'Now,' she said, 'Jim—will you pull him right
up to the door? As slowly and gently as you can.'
Reluctantly, but unable to resist the pull on his
tender nose, Angus advanced and, leaning
forward, Alice plunged the needle into the shoulder muscle with as much force as she could
muster. Thankfully she realised that she had got
through and held on firmly until the syringe
was empty.

Expecting a violent reaction, she stood quickly
back but to her surprise Angus seemed to accept
the situation with unusual docility.

'Nice work!' James's voice startled her so much
that she dropped the syringe, which he picked up
and handed it to her with an approving smile. 'I
came up just in time to hear your advice about
improving this poor fellow's accommodation.
Then I kept in the background so as not to
disturb you.'

He turned as Mr Thompson said, 'Come at last, have you? Well, Alice here has done the necessary and very well, too.'

Glowing inwardly at the reluctant praise, she said, 'Angus will need another injection tomorrow. Either I or Mr Preston will do it.'

'There you are,' James said smoothly. 'I told you she was as good as any man, didn't I?'

'That she is.' Mr Thompson grinned, a little shamefaced. Then he laughed. 'I'll pass it round at the next farmers' meeting.'

Under pretext of lack of time James and Alice declined the offer of a cup of tea and went back to their respective cars. Alice waited for James to show his displeasure at having his case taken over but, to her surprise, he said, 'You know, I was a bit nervous when I saw you just about to plunge in that injection. I thought you might have found it too tough and that Angus would probably have turned nasty.

'But you were right—I shouldn't have doubted your ability.'

She flushed at his praise. 'I thought you might have been angry.'

'Angry? With you? In any case—' his mouth twitched '—you're the boss, aren't you? Which reminds me, will you fix a date—a dinner date—during which we can have a quiet uninterrupted talk about the future?'

He paused and smiled ruefully. 'When I say "uninterrupted" I mean always excepting anything urgent. It would be nice to go outside this area, don't you think? In any of the local places we might run into Edward and Becky—I gather they've taken a shine to each other.'

James was looking keenly at her and his eyebrows rose as she laughed. 'That's good news. How did you find out?'

'Becky told Sophie who told me. Becky apparently was "over the moon", as Sophie put it. Being a bit of a matchmaker she is very hopeful and so am I. It takes off the pressure my respected sister-in-law has been putting on me.'

Alice laughed mockingly. 'Poor James. She should have realised that an eligible bachelor like you would want to be left alone to play the field in your own way.' He winced and she bit her lip, then added hastily, 'I'm sorry. Forget I said that, will you? I should have remembered—your fiancée—'

He frowned. 'Nothing to do with it. As for "playing the field", that's not for me.'

She opened her car door and as she got in he said, 'How about tomorrow evening? If you can fix things up with Carol I'll call for you about seven-thirty. Would you like me to take evening surgery? That would give you a bit more time to get ready.'

'That would be nice.' She smiled at him as she started the car. 'See you later.'

As she drove back she reflected on their conversation but could come to no satisfactory conclusion. James remained an enigma. The trouble was that one had to be so careful not to tread on dangerous ground when asking questions. But even if he had no wish to talk about

his personal life he was bound to tell her sooner
or later of his plans for the future.

For the rest of the day she was busy. The
accounts needed attention and, settling down in
her office, she immersed herself in what she
always found a disagreeable task.

Carol, bringing her a cup of tea, frowned as
she saw the pile of paperwork. 'You know, you
really should get computerised.' She laughed as
Alice shrugged off the suggestion dismissively, but
went on, 'You simply can't go on in this
old-fashioned way.'

'It's not that, entirely. I admit I don't care for
all this technology but I'm afraid of laying out
vast sums just at the moment.'

Carol shrugged. 'It would save you so much
time. Then there's this identity chip thing. That
would be a great asset to the practice. OK—no
need to frown like that. I'm talking sense.'

Alice nodded reluctantly. 'I'm beginning to
think you're right. How are you on computers?'

'A dab hand,' Carol said, laughing. 'And as for
the identity chip system we'd soon—'

'Hey! One thing at a time!' Alice paused. 'Actually, I'm going out to dinner with James tomorrow
night so I'll talk it over with him, though, of
course, if he tells me he's going back to
Australia—' Her voice faded away and she looked
at Carol hopelessly.

'Well, tomorrow night isn't far off,' said Carol
bracingly. 'Let's keep our fingers crossed.' She
picked up the cups but put them down again at
the sound of the telephone. Answering in her

usual efficient manner, she was silent for a few moments and then said, 'No, he's out on calls—yes, she's here.' Handing over the receiver she said, 'James's sister-in-law—'

Sophie was agitated. 'One of our cows—I'm worried. Can you come over? I don't like to wait for James.'

Quickly picking up her case Alice said, 'I may be some time. Can you cope?'

'Of course.' Carol's cheerful reassurance was comforting and as Alice drove away she found herself reflecting on her luck in having Carol back in her old job. She was helping to make things run smoothly even without the technology which was apparently so necessary.

As to that, even if James did return to Australia she would have to move with the times. Maybe a bank loan would provide the financial help needed.

Her spirits lifted as she pictured her surgery fitted out with all the latest equipment, then sank again as she realised how empty it would seem without James. That dismal thought was brought to an end by her arrival at her destination.

Sophie was waiting outside for her and led her quickly to the cowshed. 'The herdsman is away with flu and David has gone to see our solicitor. I do the relief milking but it's all so new to me that I wonder if we're not taking on too much. When something like this happens I'm inclined to panic.'

As they entered the cowshed she said, 'Look,

doesn't she look dreadful? And that poor little calf—only three days old.'

Alice quickly took charge. 'First of all the calf must be taken away. We must put it in another box.'

Between the two of them they managed to get the protesting little heifer settled in next door. As Alice examined the recumbent cow Sophie said fearfully, 'It isn't that awful "mad cow disease", is it?'

'Goodness, no. These are the symptoms of milk fever. It often occurs after a calving and is easy to put right. Did James do the calving?'

'Yes, and he said it was easy. This must have come on very suddenly because he looked at her this morning and said everything was OK.'

Alice nodded. 'Milk fever is a fall in the level of blood calcium and if it's caught in time can soon be treated with an injection under the skin of calcium borogluconate. You did the right thing by calling me out immediately you discovered it.'

Cheered by this praise, Sophie watched with interest as Alice began her preparations. Taking a bottle from her case she said, 'I'm going to give her four hundred millilitres—that should do the trick.' Having taken off the top, she fixed in a tube and on the other end of the tube she inserted a large needle.

Holding the bottle at shoulder level with her left hand, she pushed the needle in just under the cow's skin and watched as the liquid flowed down the tube. 'Won't take long,' she said, and stayed silent until the bottle was empty. A few minutes after she had withdrawn the needle the cow began to move and finally struggled to her feet.

Sophie said, 'That's marvellous. Shall we get her calf now?'

'No. Not just yet. In an hour or so. Get James to look at her next time he comes in and again this evening.'

Sophie looked puzzled. 'Aren't you going out to dinner with him this evening?' She hesitated and then laughed. 'I'm wrong again! It's tomorrow, isn't it?'

Alice's eyebrows rose. 'The only person around here who is able to keep a secret is James. Yes, tomorrow evening we're going to discuss the future. I'm just hoping he won't be going back to Australia.'

'Oh, I don't think he'll go back now in view of the news Janey brought him.'

Alice tried to speak casually. 'I see—well—actually, I don't see. What was the news or don't you know?'

'Oh, yes, I know but—' Sophie laughed. 'I don't think I'd better tell you. James says I get everything wrong and it's all so complicated. I'll leave it to him to tell you.'

'He probably won't,' Alice said drily, 'and if it's anything to do with his personal life I haven't the right to ask him.'

Sophie shrugged. 'You won't have to. He's bound to tell you so don't worry.'

But Alice found that she was even more worried than before. If James was bound to tell her it could only mean one thing.

Utterly depressed, she was glad when evening surgery was so busy that she was able to put all her fears to the back of her mind. She had just finished operating on a dog with a large hernia and after putting in the last stitches she stood back and waited while Carol installed him in a recovering cage.

'Coffee time,' she called as she put on the kettle and sighed as she heard the outer door open. She supposed it was a last-minute client and on opening the waiting-room door she was surprised to see Janey smiling at her.

'I can see I've come at the right time. May I have a coffee with you?' She paused as Alice waved her inside and added, 'Afterwards I'd like to have a word with you.'

The conversation was general at first, with Janey regaling them with anecdotes of her work as an assistant vet in Australia. Although she was not boastful it soon became evident that she was extremely capable and very up to date. Then, coffee finished, Carol tactfully disappeared and Janey said, 'You look worried, Alice. What's up?'

Alice forced a smile. 'Nothing really, except that I can't possibly imagine what you want to talk to me about. I can only hazard a guess that it's something to do with James. Probably that he's going back to Australia and that, of course, will make things difficult for me.'

'You do look on the black side, don't you?' Janey shook her head and laughed. 'If that were the case I wouldn't be the one to tell you. I'm just here to give you a hint or two. I happen to know that you're going out with James tomorrow evening—don't frown—Sophie told me, of course. You probably think that has nothing to do with me but it has.'

She paused. 'I came over here to give him some news. Personal news which has had a great effect on him. You know about the terrible accident when his mother and his fiancée were killed, don't you?'

Alice nodded. 'Sophie told me but when I mentioned it to James he said she had got the details all wrong.'

'Well, she had but then so had we all. But now the truth has come out and it's made a new man of James.'

Utterly confused, Alice stared in amazement. 'What on earth has such a personal thing got to do with me?'

Janey gazed back at her with a half-smile. 'Well, James will tell you that. All I'm suggesting is that you give him every chance to tell you his story. Don't put him off by saying it has nothing to do with you—because it has.'

Alice shook her head. 'I can't see how but I'll take your advice. I can't help feeling, though, that what is apparently good news for him will be bad news for me.' She got up from the table. 'I must look at my patient to make sure he's OK.'

Janey pushed back her chair. 'May I come with you? I'm professionally interested, you know.'

Casting a quick look round the surgery as they went to the recovery room, she said bluntly, 'You're not very up to date, are you?'

Alice winced. 'Well, I haven't got all the very latest things but—' She shrugged and added defensively, 'Things have been a bit difficult since my father's death.'

'Of course.' Janey sounded sympathetic but Alice smarted under her implied criticism and added coolly, 'Some of this new equipment is so expensive that, taking into account the comparatively rare occasions when it would be used, it hardly justifies the outlay.'

Janey fell silent, evidently deciding that she had said enough and, after watching Alice examine her patient, she said goodbye. Alone in the recovery room, anxiously watching and testing for signs of the dog's return to consciousness, Alice refused to allow herself any more useless speculation about James.

At last, after gently pinching her patient's toes, she saw a little jerk and knew that the reflexes were coming back. Satisfied, she left the door open and settled down to wait until full consciousness returned.

Next morning, having handed him over to his master when he came to fetch him after surgery, Alice sat drinking coffee on her own as Carol had gone to do some shopping. Now, at last, she allowed her thoughts to dwell on the evening ahead.

She must, she told herself sternly, anticipate the worst and keep a strict guard on her emotions when James told her that he was going to leave. All she could hope for was that he would not break his agreement and go before his six months engagement was up. That would be too awful. Once more she would be on her own and the search for his replacement would begin all over again.

That was the practical side but worse than anything was the knowledge that she would never see him again. That thought took precedence over all and gradually tears flowed uncontrollably as she visualised the dark future without the man she loved.

Suddenly the door opened and, hastily wiping her eyes, she saw as though in a misty dream James coming towards her. All at once she felt herself enveloped firmly in his arms and, turning, she clung to him. There seemed no need for words but at last she looked up and as their eyes met she felt a sudden shock. No man had ever looked at her like that.

Slowly he lowered his head and kissed her trembling mouth. Still not speaking, he released her, turned and went into the office.

A moment later Carol came in and with a quick glance at Alice's tear-stained face she said, 'It's about time you had a good cry. You've been bottling things up far too long. Thank goodness you're going out tonight. It will do you the world of good. Are you upset about that poor little dog we had to put to sleep during surgery?'

Thankful for this unexpected reason for her emotional breakdown, Alice nevertheless felt guilty as she nodded assent.

She felt even more hypocritical as she added, 'Well, yes, in a way,' and excused herself on the grounds that it was the only solution to an embarrassing situation.

Carol said calmly, 'A cup of good strong coffee will soon put you right. As for this evening, you know I'll stand in for you and won't call on either of you if at all possible. There could be nothing more infuriating than being called away in the middle of a romantic dinner date.'

Alice flushed and with a quick glance at the open door of the office she said sharply, 'Romantic? Who said anything about that? We're just going to discuss the future of this practice.'

Carol shrugged and laughed as James emerged from the office and said smilingly, 'I heard the magic word "coffee". A very good idea.'

It was comforting and as though to cover up Alice's embarrassment, he said, 'It's always sad when we have to put animals to sleep. We're in this profession to heal whenever possible but there are times when in order to save suffering—' He shrugged sadly. 'No one who loves animals ever gets hardened to it.'

After that the conversation became general and James said, 'I have a suggestion. Why don't you take the afternoon off, Alice?' He turned to Carol. 'I haven't anything on this afternoon so you can always get me at my brother's house. And of course I'll come in and do evening surgery.' He smiled. 'That OK with you, Alice?'

She nodded thankfully. A good rest before going out to dinner would help her gain strength to face up to whatever blow fate was about to deal her.

CHAPTER NINE

HER beautiful hair falling in soft waves over her shoulders, her low-cut dress clinging to her slim figure, Alice made a picture that made James gasp softly when he came to fetch her that evening.

Off duty, he seemed another man—settling her carefully into his car and treating her as though she was fragile and very feminine. It was a new experience for Alice and at first she found it delightful but after being asked for the third time if she was quite comfortable, she dissolved into laughter.

'Honestly, James. I'm not made of sugar. I'm a pretty tough veterinary surgeon, you know.'

He glanced at her quickly and grinned. 'Pretty, yes, but not tough. And tonight you are a dream of beauty.'

She flushed but said nothing and as they drove along she glanced at him curiously. He did seem a different man. That hint of inward brooding had gone and he was smiling to himself as though a burden had been lifted off his shoulders. It was tantalising and she found it hard to refrain from questioning him. It was not until they were seated at table in the restaurant of a country hotel that he began to talk.

'This place was recommended to me by my

brother. He and Sophie took Janey here a few days ago.'

Her curiosity aroused, Alice sipped reflectively at her glass of wine and said, 'Janey intrigues me. She seems to be on some kind of mission. Has she brought news that pleases you?' She hesitated and added almost apologetically, 'I'm only asking because there's something different about you this evening.'

'Well—' He smiled across at her. 'That could be because you've turned my head by the way you look but, yes, Janey is on a kind of mission. She has brought me news—good news that— well—I don't quite know where to begin.' He gazed at her steadily and her heart began to beat unevenly.

Trying to calm herself, she concentrated on his appearance. Dressed formally in a well-cut suit, James looked devastatingly handsome and as he gazed reflectively into his glass her whole being yearned towards him. Suddenly he looked up.

'The news was very personal and with it came an offer. A business offer from my father that could, if I wished to take it up, change my whole way of life.' He picked up his knife and fork and began to eat as though he had said all that he intended. It was more than Alice could stand.

'Well, go on. Aren't you going to tell me any more?'

Then she bit her lip as he looked at her so strangely that she felt rebuked. She shrugged. 'Sorry. Obviously it's nothing to do with me. I'm just glad that you have had good news.'

'Ah—but it has a lot to do with you. More than you realise. Listen—' He leant across the table and as their eyes met she felt a chill of apprehension.

'My father is about to sell his practice in Perth. His new wife—' his lip curled scornfully '—doesn't like being a busy vet's wife. Not her thing at all. She wants to travel and as he is entirely under her spell he says he wants to be free to travel with her. He's not short of money and she has plenty of her own. With the sale of the practice or even without it they can enjoy complete freedom from the ties of everyday work.'

He frowned down at his plate, then, looking up suddenly, he added, 'My father has given me first choice.'

'"First choice"?' Alice looked blank. 'First choice of what?'

'Why, the practice of course,' he said impatiently. 'If I turn it down then Janey and a friend will buy it between them. She's very keen but doesn't think she has much of a chance.'

Alice's hand shook as she picked up her glass. Her mouth was dry and it was difficult to speak. At last in a strained voice she said, 'Well—all I can say is good luck and—and—' she drew a long breath '—goodbye.'

'You take it for granted that I will take up my father's offer?' He looked pale and rather grim but she forced a smile. 'It seems obvious. A practice handed to you on a plate.' She swallowed hard. 'When do you want to go?'

He frowned, shaking his head as though confused. 'Alice, have you forgotten my offer to you—a partnership in return for financial help?' He paused. 'You seem certain that I will leave—almost indifferent about the whole thing. But my roots are here in England. My offer still stands.'

She saw a small pulse beating in his temple as he added, 'There's another reason—the most important one of all—why I prefer to stay here but I won't go into that just yet. It's obviously not the right moment.'

Alice sat very still, the food on her plate forgotten. Once again he was being mysterious. She would have to know more before telling him how much she wanted him to stay. She said slowly, 'This other reason—is it the personal one you mentioned?'

He nodded reluctantly and then fell silent. Alice was left with the impression that she was being too curious. Resentment overcame her sadness and she almost welcomed the ringing tone of James's mobile phone.

'Oh, damn, damn—' He pulled it out. 'Carol? Yes. What's up?' He listened carefully, then handed the instrument over to Alice. 'For you. Looks like a Caesarean.'

She took a few more details from Carol and, handing back the instrument, said, 'Poor girl. She hates calling us back. She's done what she can but only a Caesar will save the bitch now.'

They drove back in complete silence and Alice's thoughts were bitter. So bitter that when, on arrival at the surgery, James said, 'Would you like me to operate? Your beautiful dress—' she snapped at him.

'My overall will cover that.' Seeing the stricken look on his face, she felt instant remorse. 'I'm sorry—I'm a bit jumpy. I would like you to stay and help me.' She turned to Carol. 'Look—you've done all you could. You deserve a break. It's been a long day for you. We can manage now.'

Carol nodded gratefully. Pointing to the message pad she said, 'Here's the number to ring when you've done the op. I've told the owners you would be operating and they're very anxious. Don't bother to tidy up afterwards. I'll come in early tomorrow morning.' She turned at the door. 'Everything is sterilised and ready.'

'That girl is a treasure.' James pulled on his overall and then he picked up the little mongrel and placed her gently on the table. 'God!' he exclaimed. 'She's in a bad way. Must have been straining all day.'

Alice nodded as she looked down at her patient. Eyes half-closed and her swollen body limp and almost lifeless, she seemed to have given up her hopeless struggle. 'I'll just feel the cervix,' she said and as the little bitch became aware of the gentle examination she opened her eyes and gave a sad little whimper. 'Well, all that straining has been useless. There's nothing in the passage so that means a dead puppy.'

Alice turned to James who had taken charge of the anaesthetic machine. 'It's risky to operate in her state of exhaustion but she'll die in misery if I don't.'

They worked in silence and the first puppy—a very large one—was lifted out dead. Alice said, 'There is one more—maybe two. I think they're alive.'

Half an hour later the still-unconscious bitch was placed in a warm recovery cage with her two puppies in the one next door. Studying her breathing, Alice said, 'I'll give her a heart stimulant,' and turned to find James holding the filled syringe.

Suddenly her whole being was enveloped in a surge of love. It had been wonderful having him there sustaining and helping her in every way. She must stop doubting him and accept whatever decision he made. Then she heard him say softly, 'She can't be left yet. I'll stay with her if you like. You look tired.'

Alice shook her head. 'A better idea would be for us to have a cup of tea. I'll put the kettle on.'

He smiled and went to fetch a couple of chairs from the surgery. When she brought the tea he laughed as they settled themselves by the recovery cages.

'What a strange ending to what Carol called a "romantic evening".' He nodded smilingly. 'Yes, I heard what she said. I also heard your indignant denial that there was no question of romance. Unfortunately, as our evening together was cut short I haven't had the opportunity of proving which statement was correct.'

He paused, his eyes fixed on her in a way that was so disturbing that she turned towards the cage holding the puppies and pretended to examine

them. He gave a rueful laugh, 'Don't worry. I'm
not going to take advantage of our situation here.
It's hardly the place or the time.'

Suddenly Alice felt a great desire for sleep. So
great that she almost fell off her chair and as
James put out his arm to save her she looked up
at him with half-closed eyes. She said slowly, 'I'm
suddenly all in. I think I must take advantage of
your offer and leave you to watch over the bitch.'

He nodded with such tenderness in his eyes that
she knew if she stayed much longer she would
end up in his arms. Trying to pull herself together
she said, 'I should think another hour of watching
would be enough.'

He got up and held out his hand to steady
her. 'Meanwhile I'll walk you back to the house.
Come along.'

She had a brief word with her mother and in
a very short time Alice was in bed and asleep.

In the morning, on going into the recovery room,
she found a note left by James. 'Left here at two
a.m. Bitch fully conscious, puppies OK.' After
making certain that all was progressing favourably
she began her morning surgery. At coffee-time
James came in, looking surprisingly bright and
cheerful in spite of his short night.

Alice smiled at him. 'The bitch and her puppies
have gone home. The owners have promised to
follow my directions and are full of gratitude.'

Carol put the coffee-mugs on the table and said
ruefully, 'That's rewarding, of course, but I hated
having have to break up your evening.' She

glanced at Alice. 'You get so little time off. Still, perhaps next time you'll be luckier.'

A shadow crossed Alice's face. Most likely another time would be a dinner of farewell—a thought that caused such a pang in her heart that she hurriedly took up her coffee in order to hide from James's searching gaze. He said calmly, '"Next time luckier"? Let's hope you're right.

'Talking of luck—I'm going to need some on my next job. A stallion to be castrated. He should have been "done" long ago—now he's fully grown and dangerous. Mr Benson was putting some hay in his box and stumbled over some small obstacle. It startled the stallion and he bit a chunk out of his unfortunate master's arm.

'It was purely a nervous reaction, of course, but—' he shrugged '—no option, I'm afraid.'

He went on, 'I can see you're interested, Alice, but it's one of those jobs that—' He shook his head. 'You wouldn't be welcome there, you know. Mr Benson is a bit old-fashioned and wouldn't like a woman even looking on.' He laughed. 'Come to that, I don't think I like the idea either so perhaps I'm old-fashioned, too.'

Alice bristled and said scornfully, 'Men! They're so squeamish! "Cutting" a stallion—well, I castrate cats and dogs, Carol cleans up the most revolting messes, yet I can't even be present at—'

James chuckled. 'You know, I think you're right. Working in this all-women practice I'm beginning to see the feminine side of things. All the same, I can't overrule Mr Benson's scruples. He's one of those "delicate-minded" farmers I mentioned and which caused your mother so much hilarity.'

He got up. 'So I'm off now to do the stallion, then on to Willow Farm to inject some pigs and after that to treat some scouring calves. See you later.'

When he had gone Carol said, 'I'm dying of curiosity. You two had quite a long time together before I had to call you out yesterday evening. Did you learn anything about his plans?'

Alice hesitated and said slowly, 'He gave me some news—the news that Janey brought. It shook me to the core.' She stopped and then, with an impulsive rush, she said, 'Listen to this.'

When she had finished Carol said, 'That's a bit of a bombshell. And you say he hasn't yet decided what to do?'

'No. He said it depended on something else—something he has yet to tell me.'

Carol looked thoughtful. 'I wonder—' She stopped and, as Alice waited, she said slowly, 'It would break your heart if he decided to take up his father's offer, wouldn't it?' As she saw the stricken look on Alice's face, she said quickly, 'Sorry. I shouldn't have asked that.'

Fighting back the hot tears that threatened to fall, Alice went into the office and tried to get her feelings under control. She mustn't give way like this. If the worst should happen she must take it calmly and hide her grief just as she had when Edward had announced his engagement.

Not that there was any comparison between the two situations. It was ludicrous to compare infatuation with love—real love that filled her whole being with pain at the thought of it never being returned. At the sound of voices she rose and went into the surgery to investigate.

Looking up, Carol said, 'A badly injured pigeon. I don't think—' She stopped and indicated a small boy who was watching her anxiously. 'Well, you have a look.' She turned to the child. 'This lady is a veterinary surgeon so she'll know what to do.'

In the cardboard carton the bird lay very still and a quick examination told her enough. She was on the point of giving her verdict when the boy said, 'You'll be able to make him better, won't you? I found him and I want to keep him. I've never had a pet, see?'

Alice looked at him compassionately then shook her head.

'I'm sorry, very sorry, but he has just died.'

To her dismay the child burst into tears. 'I don't believe it. He was alive when I picked him up.'

Alice nodded. 'Yes, but he's been shot—badly shot—he was dying when you picked him up. Well, you gave him a better death than he would have had lying in the open. See how he just went to sleep lying on the soft grass you put in the box.'

Comforted, the boy went away clutching a bar of chocolate and the two girls smiled at each other. Carol laughed. 'We're both soft touches. Perhaps it's our maternal instinct—' She stopped as James came through the door.

'Finished,' he announced. 'Mr Benson changed his mind about the stallion. Decided he'd try to sell him to a stud. So I made short work of the pigs and calves and I've come back just in time to take you out to lunch.' Seeing Alice's hesitation, he said firmly, 'Now, don't make excuses. We've still got some more talking to do.'

She was just about to accept when Carol said, 'Alice—Mr Sanders is coming in to show you how his three-legged Labrador is getting on. Had you forgotten?'

'Oh, my goodness, yes—thank you for reminding me.' She turned to James. 'Sorry, but you see how it is.'

He shrugged regretfully. 'Can't be helped. Never mind, another time.' He paused. 'I'd like to see the progress of our three-legged friend so I'll stay.'

Half an hour later Mr Sanders arrived and lolloping along behind him came Bess, waving her tail and going from one to the other as they admired and petted her. Mr Sanders looked down at her proudly. 'See, her coat is just beginning to grow back and she doesn't seem at all worried about her unsteady walk. In any case it's getting better all the time. I give her a little more exercise every day.'

Alice nodded. 'I think by the time her coat is back she'll be able to run beside your wife's chair.'

'Even before that, perhaps—why, she even tried to chase after a cat that had got into our garden yesterday. Of course she nearly fell over but she didn't mind. Wagged her tail at me as though to say she'd soon see intruders off.'

It was a happy reunion and when, at last, Mr

Sanders left James looked at his watch. 'Too late for lunch. I think I'll go and see what my sister-in-law can produce. What about you two?'

'A sandwich and coffee,' Alice said with a laugh. 'You're welcome to join us.'

He shook his head and grinned. 'Not enough for me. I'm hungry. See you later.'

As they sat over their snack lunch Carol said thoughtfully, 'It really seems that Fate is against you and James ever having time to talk and get things sorted out. Somehow or other you've got to arrange a meeting—one that won't be interrupted by an emergency. How are you going to do that?'

'I don't know.' Alice frowned. 'It seems hopeless. Perhaps James will think something up. It's really up to him, isn't it?'

'Yes, it is—' Carol looked suddenly cheerful '—and if I know James he'll work it somehow.'

Evening surgery was uneventful and Alice went to bed early, hoping to make up for lost sleep. Almost as soon as her head touched the pillow she drifted off, only to be shaken awake by her mother's agitated voice.

'Alice—Alice—Angel is missing! I can't find her anywhere.'

'Missing?' She turned to look at her bedside clock. 'Half-past eleven—what on earth?'

Mrs Norton went to the window overlooking the large garden. 'I put her out there soon after you came up. She always runs around for about a quarter of an hour before coming upstairs with me. But she seems to have disappeared. I've called and called, been out and searched and found the gate open. I'm sure I shut it but even if it's ever left open by mistake she never goes out on her own.'

Jumping out of bed, Alice joined her mother at the window but the garden lay silent under a full moon. Mrs Norton was on the point of tears. 'What can we do?'

Hastily pulling on some clothes, Alice said, 'I'll get the car out and see if I can find her. She can't have gone far. You'd better stay here in case she comes back of her own accord.'

The lane was deserted and Alice drove along at a snail's pace, turning her lights onto the most likely places and dreading to see a small white body lying in the gutter. After half an hour she pulled up in defeat. There was nothing for it but to return and hope that Angel had come home on her own. She found her mother being comforted by Carol who looked up as Alice stood in the doorway. 'I heard the commotion and came down. What news?'

Alice shook her head despondently. 'I've covered several miles but there's no sign.'

Carol picked up the kettle. 'Some tea while we're waiting. There was a telephone call for you when you were out so I put it through to James and told him what was happening here. He rang back to say that the call was one of those trivial things that could wait till the morning. He's coming over here to see if he can help. Listen—' She stopped and Alice heard the welcome sound of James's car.

Filled with gratitude, she went to meet him. A few words of explanation and he said, 'I'll go over to the police station and come back by another route.' He glanced over her shoulder. 'Your mother is in shock. Will she be OK with Carol? If so I'd like you to come with me. Angel knows you better than she knows me and is more likely to respond to your voice.'

Alice had a few words with Carol and then, seated in James's car, she puzzled over that open gate. 'James, do you think—?' She voiced her fears. 'Do you think Angel has been stolen?'

James shrugged. 'It's possible, but not likely. She's not a valuable bitch. Anyway, who would come into the garden in full moonlight and make off with her so silently? Did your mother hear her bark?'

'She didn't say but I'm sure if she did she'd have been out in the garden like a shot to investigate.'

Soon they were at the police station and the officer on duty took all the details and promised to let them know if the dog was brought in. Back in the car, they resumed their search which proved fruitless and so, tired and worried, they drove back to find Carol on her own.

'I persuaded your mother to go to bed. I gave her something to calm her down and promised to wake her if you were successful—which obviously you are not. Sit down now and have a cup of tea.'

James shook his head. 'I'd better not. I'll get up early to make enquiries all round. Better leave the gate open so that Angel can get in if she comes back on her own.'

Several times during the short night Alice got up and went outside, calling quietly but with no success. Next morning she found Carol putting up a large notice in the waiting-room and helped her to print out some more for general distribution. When James came in he said, 'I'm putting off all non-urgent calls till tomorrow but I have to go over to Mr Walker's farm to cleanse a cow. I'll be as quick as I can.'

When he had gone Alice said, 'Thank goodness there don't seem to be many people in the waiting-room. I just don't feel at my best.'

Luckily the cases were mostly routine and she was able to find time to tell the clients about Angel so that they could join in the search. At last, when the door closed behind the last one she said to Carol, 'I think I'll take my coffee into the house and have it with Ma. Call me back if necessary.'

Her mother looked preoccupied and in answer to Alice's query she said, 'I've been searching my mind to see if I can find a clue to Angel's disappearance. I remember taking her with me when I went shopping. We ended up outside the post office where I met one of your father's old clients—Mrs White. We stood there talking. She admired Angel and said she was lucky to have been taken into a vet's family.'

Alice frowned. 'Was there anybody nearby who might have overheard you talking?'

Mrs Norton shook her head. 'Not that I remember. Wait, though—let me concentrate. Yes, I think there was a man standing by the post box.

Youngish, scruffy-looking—you know—long hair, torn jacket, several necklaces. He didn't seem interested, however. When Mrs White and I parted I think he went into the post office.'

Alice shrugged. 'I don't suppose—' She stopped. 'You said that Mrs White said how lucky Angel was to have been adopted by a vet's family. Could that man have heard that?'

Mrs Norton shrugged. 'It's possible, Mrs White is a bit deaf and one has to talk rather loudly.

'Oh, my goodness, I've remembered another thing: she asked me if Angel had been difficult to house-train and I said, no, not at all. I'd got her into a regular routine during the day and at night I just put her out into the garden for about a quarter of an hour and she went right through till morning. Alice—' she stared at her daughter in dismay '—do you think that man came along and stole her?'

The idea was frightening and Alice was nonplussed for a moment. Then she said, 'Let's ring Mrs Sadler at the post office and ask if she remembers him. She might even know him.'

Luckily, the post office was not busy and Mrs Sadler was able to chat. 'Yes, I remember him because I nearly called you back, only you'd gone out of sight. Quite a coincidence really. He asked me if I knew the address of the local vet. I hadn't time to tell him exactly where you live so I gave him the book, told him your name and left him to look up the address himself.' She paused. 'Why do you want to know?'

Alice told her and Mrs Sadler was shocked.

'That dear little dog—what a shame. Of course she might have strayed again. Anyway, I'll ask all the local people who come in here.'

Deep in thought, Alice replaced the receiver and after talking some more with her mother she went back to the surgery. She was just about to tell Carol of her suspicions when James walked in. 'All done,' he said briskly. 'Now I'm at your disposal. Any suggestions?'

'Well, my mother has come up with something that looks rather ominous,' said Alice, and when she had finished he looked grim. She said, 'What do you think? Not strayed but stolen?'

He nodded slowly. 'It looks like it.'

They sat in gloomy silence for a while then, suddenly, James came alive. 'I've got it! It all fits. Listen—' He collected his thoughts. 'I was cleansing that cow when Mr Walker started grumbling as usual. I don't often pay much attention to him—he's always got some grievance—but now I remember what he was moaning about.

'He said those New Age travellers were back in another of his fields, next to the one from which they had been evicted. Remember we all thought that perhaps it was from there that Angel had run away? Now, that scruffy-looking man was standing by the pillar-box while your mother and her old—rather deaf—friend were talking about Angel and Angel herself was sitting patiently waiting.

'When he heard that the dog was put out in the garden last thing at night he went into the post office to get the address of the local vet.

Then all he had to do was to wait around a bit till Mrs Norton opened the door to let Angel out.

'When the door was shut he crept into the garden and grabbed her. I don't suppose she had time to bark. She was probably shoved very quickly into a sack or something. In any case, she probably was terrified of him—remember how she had been treated.' He stopped, then added grimly, 'It isn't even a case of theft. The dog belongs to him. All the same—' he got up '—I'm going over to the travellers' encampment to see what I can do.'

Alice said quickly, 'I'll come with you. Oh, don't look like that. Of course I must.'

He glared at her for a minute. 'I don't like the idea. Things might get a bit ugly. Oh, all right. I can see you are determined. Let's go.'

The entrance to the field had been blocked by a huge lorry and so James left his car in the lane. As Alice got out he said, 'Yes, perhaps you'll be safer with me than left alone in the car.'

She laughed quietly. 'I don't think these people are violent.' She pointed as they squeezed past the lorry. 'See that man over there? He fits my mother's description.'

Catching sight of them, the man came towards them and asked suspiciously, 'Wotcher want?'

James laughed. 'Well, we havent come to join you but we're making enquiries about a small white dog. It's been missing since yesterday. We think it's been stolen.'

'Stolen, is it?' the man laughed unpleasantly.

'Not stolen by me. Stolen by you. I've taken her back. She's my dog.'

Alice gasped in dismay but James said coolly, 'In that case I'll have to report you for cruelty. When we found her she was in a very bad state. Cigarette burns, bruises from kicks. I'm a vet and I could get you into serious trouble.'

For the first time the man looked uneasy. 'You've got no proof. She's all right now.'

'Of course. We've treated her.' Suddenly James's voice lost its harshness. 'I know she's legally your dog but I'd like to buy her from you. What do you say?'

There's was a moment's silence, then the man said scornfully, 'Wanna buy Flo? That little mongrel?' He shrugged. 'It'll cost you.'

'Yes. How much?'

James took out his wallet and Alice, alarmed, said quickly, 'Careful, James,' and moved forward a step, expecting it to be snatched from him, but her anxious glance was intercepted.

'Think we're all thieves, don't you? Well, we're not.' The man turned to James. 'A hundred pounds, cash.'

'Done!' James counted out the notes but did not hand the money over. 'Let's get the dog first.' They were led across the field towards a battered-looking caravan—and there was Angel, tied to a wheel on a very short rope. Tail down, whimpering and tugging at the rope, she looked the picture of misery.

As they drew near Alice called her name and instantly there was a transformation. Barking hysterically and jumping up and down, she was in danger of strangling herself. 'Shut up, Flo.' Her former owner bent down to untie her. 'Shut up or I'll—'

'Oh, no, you won't.' James took over. 'She's our dog now and don't you forget it.' He handed Angel over to Alice's welcoming arms and then pushed the money into the man's hand. For a few moments he stood gazing around. 'Quite a few dogs here. A poor, mangy lot, too. I think the RSPCA might—'

With a muttered, 'Go to hell,' the man made off quickly.

As James took the wheel of his car Alice tried to calm Angel down. Wild with joy, she was almost impossible to control and at last, turning her head from side to side in an effort to avoid the little dog's exuberant licking, she said, 'Angel—if you don't settle down I'll start calling you Flo!'

James burst out laughing. 'Actually, it's not a bad name. More sensible than "Angel".' He glanced sideways. 'Here, you drive and I'll take her over.'

Alice shook her head. 'It's all right. She's calming down. By the way, that hundred pounds you paid for her—I'll refund you as soon as we get back.'

He shook his head firmly. 'No, certainly not. And you're not to tell your mother. We'll just say we came to an agreement. I'd like to give her to your mother—she's been very good to me so let me have that pleasure. Promise?'

Alice nodded but her heart sank. It sounded as

though he was talking about a farewell gift. She said quietly, 'You're very secretive, aren't you? It's not a trait I care for.'

His hands tightened on the steering wheel. He said harshly, 'God! That's cruel! You must try to understand. I am not the secretive type at all. I've had to hide my feelings for a long time but as soon as I can find the opportunity I'm going to explain everything. Finding the opportunity is the difficult thing.

'What about this? As soon as we've handed Angel back to your mother, come and have a snack lunch with me. It doesn't matter where— a quiet corner in the local pub perhaps.' Guiding the car into the driveway he turned off the engine and, looking at her steadily, said again, 'Please.'

Alice's spirits rose as she met his eyes. She smiled. 'OK. I'd like that.'

'Right! Now let's go and make your mother happy.'

It was a moving reunion and Alice's eyes were misty as she saw her mother's joy. Then the story was told but no mention of payment was made. Mrs Norton, covered with Angel's loving caresses, was hardly able to take it all in and it was only necessary to give her the bare facts. At last, having decided that Angel must be starving, Mrs Norton began preparing a meal for her and James said quietly, 'We're just going to the local for a quick snack. We've got some things to talk over. We'll see you later.'

CHAPTER TEN

As soon as they were seated at a table hidden away from the main part of the room and had given their orders, James began to talk. But it was only of trivial things and, at last, Alice lost patience.

'James—you're holding out on me. You said you were waiting for the right opportunity to tell me something personal. Well, here's the opportunity.'

'Yes, yes, I know—' He ran his hand through his hair. 'I'm a bit nervous, that's all. I don't quite know where to begin.'

'You nervous? I don't believe it.'

'Well,' he started, 'there are several things—' There was a long pause then, drawing a long breath, he began again slowly. 'I'll start with something which has troubled me for a long time. I've been suffering from a bad conscience about the accident that caused the death of my mother and my fiancée.

'I should never have let Amanda drive my mother to the airport when she—my fiancée— was in such a state of fury. We had had a tremendous row. I had just found out that she was carrying on with another man—a former friend of mine—and I charged her with it just before she left.

164

'She denied it, of course, but I had proof. She was shaking with rage and threw her engagement ring back at me and ran off in near hysterics. I was so angry that I went out and had a drink, forgetting that she was in no state to drive.

'She crashed the car—with fatal results. After that I felt that I could never trust myself with regard to women. That, in fact, I was bad for them. Admittedly Amanda had betrayed me but I had killed her by choosing the wrong time to have it out with her.' He was silent for a moment. 'Do you understand? Wouldn't you have felt the same?'

Alice nodded slowly. 'Yes, I think I would. Go on.'

He looked at her gratefully and after another long breath he continued. 'Well, now I've had this burden lifted from my shoulders. Janey brought a letter from my father, as you know, and after the offer of his practice he went on to give me some news that he said would put my mind at rest.

'He was the only one who knew how I felt about the accident. In fact, he had blamed me himself and said he never wanted to see me again.' James paused, his eyes darkening as though he was reliving the trauma of the past. Suddenly, his shoulders lifted and his whole expression changed.

'The man with whom she had been having an affair, unbeknown to me, had brought his dog—badly injured in an accident—to my father who had, against all odds, managed to save it. He was so grateful that he compared the accident to his dog with the fatal crash in our family.

'To my father's astonishment, he said that he was responsible for both and told him that after Amanda—my fiancée—had left me she had gone to him and told him she had broken off her engagement to me. Apparently she had put on an act with me and was jubilant about being free at last. It was then that quite callously he had informed her that he no longer loved her and that their affair was over.

'Her reaction—quite genuine this time—had been terrible. He had given her a drink to calm her but she had left, threatening to do away with herself. So whether the crash was deliberate or caused by her emotional state no one will ever know.' James stopped and took the hand that Alice reached to him.

'Your poor mother,' she said softly. 'An innocent victim.' She paused. 'I think that must have hurt you most of all.'

'Yes,' he said. 'It did. My love—such as it was—died as soon as I learned Amanda was deceiving me.'

Gradually, as she withdrew her hand, a wave of sadness overwhelmed her. She longed to put her arms round him and share his joy at being acquitted of mistaken guilt but the prospect that opened before her was dark. She said, 'So now you can accept your father's offer and go back to Australia.' It was a statement more than a question and James stopped in the middle of lifting his glass and stared at her incredulously.

'Is that what you think I ought to do?'

'I—I, no—I just took it for granted.'

'Do you want me to go?'

She swallowed hard. 'What a question! Of course I don't but surely it would be more to your advantage to take over an established practice? Here—well, all you would receive for a lot of money would be a partnership.'

'Money doesn't come into it,' he said shortly, and his next words were so low that she hardly heard them. 'Would you miss me if I left?'

She drew a long breath. 'Yes, of course I would.' Then, afraid of betraying her real feelings, she added, 'It would be difficult to replace you.'

Suddenly the atmosphere between them grew chilled and distant. Reflecting on her seemingly indifferent words, Alice wanted desperately to take them back, but it was too late.

Pushing his plate aside, James drained his glass and said evenly, 'Janey is thinking of going back in a fortnight's time and she would like me to give her my decision by then. I wouldn't leave you in the lurch, even if I decide to go, so my father would have to wait till my six months here is up.' He paused. 'I wonder if you get my meaning when I say it all depends on you.'

Suddenly it was all too much to grasp. Alice shook her head angrily. 'I really don't know what you're talking about. I wish you wouldn't be so mysterious. It's actually nothing to do with me. You must make your own decision.' She got up from the table. 'I must go back to the surgery— lots of things to do.' She rose from the table. 'Thank you for the lunch.'

It was difficult to be cheerful and helpful during

evening surgery. Usually tactful when dealing with clients who were failing to give enough care to the welfare of their pets or those who were so indulgent that they were actually doing harm by overfeeding them, she found herself in danger of losing her temper.

Luckily Carol's warning glances held her back from giving sharp replies to what were obviously foolish questions and gradually she gained control of herself. Rather shamefacedly she closed the door behind the last client and turned to Carol, who said quietly, 'Well—you're either in love or heading for a nervous breakdown. Personally I think it's the former.'

'I rather think I need a holiday,' Alice said evasively and, avoiding Carol's sympathetic gaze, she added with a rueful smile, 'As that isn't possible I'll have to see what a few early nights will do.'

'Well, why don't you talk it over with James?' Carol said quietly. 'He might come up with another solution.'

After Carol had left, Alice pondered over her suggestion that love was the reason for the state of nerves to which she had given way during this evening's surgery. If it was so apparent to others, something must be done about it. In future she must disguise it better; put on an act and pretend that James's probable departure meant very little to her.

She had done it before with Edward—surely she could manage to hide her feelings once more. Ah, but that was so completely different that she knew it would be almost impossible. She shook her head despondently. Nevertheless she must try and, filled with resolution, she locked up and set off briskly for the house.

It was raining as she walked across the paved path and she hurried to escape the downpour. Suddenly the headlights of a car swept across her and she slipped and fell on her side on the hard surface. Shocked, she tried to get up but her head was swimming and she had to stay there for a few moments before making another attempt.

Then, thankfully, she heard James's voice. 'Wait—I'm coming. Don't try to get up.'

He was beside her almost immediately and she said, 'I'm all right—just a bit shaken up.' He raised her gently to her feet and she felt herself cradled in his arms. As her strength returned, she said, 'I don't think I've broken anything. It's just my wrist—I fell on it—I think it's sprained.'

'Let's get you indoors—no, don't attempt to walk. I'll carry you.'

Before she could protest she was lifted off her feet and in his strong arms she felt, for a moment, as though she was in heaven. Once in the house he laid her gently on a sofa and smiled down at her. 'Now, let's have a look at that wrist.' She held it out and he examined it carefully. When inadvertently she winced he nodded slowly. 'It's not a sprain. It's broken, I'm afraid. You'll have to get it set and put in plaster.'

'Oh, how awful! My right wrist. My work— how can I—?' She stopped as the door opened and her mother came in. Almost weeping, she said, 'Ma—what am I going to do? I've broken my right wrist.'

Dismayed, they stared at each other and then James said calmly, 'Let's deal with the shock first. A cup of hot sweet tea and then we'll—' He felt her wrist again. 'Actually, as you know, I could set this myself but I don't think I'd better. When you feel a bit stronger I'll take you to the hospital.'

It was not until much later that Alice, her wrist set in plaster right up her arm and down to the knuckles of her hand, realised the full significance of her unfortunate accident.

She looked down at the sling encasing her right arm and then across at James. 'Well, first of all I must thank you for all your help but—' She shook her head in dismay. 'Six weeks out of action! I won't be able to do anything—examine patients, do the simplest operation or even give injections.'

He nodded compassionately. 'That's true, but don't worry. I've thought it all out. As you know, Janey is a fully qualified vet. In my father's practice she is in charge of the small animal surgery. She can very well do your work for you. In fact, I'm pretty sure she'll welcome the opportunity.'

'But you told me she was thinking of returning to Australia in about a fortnight.'

'We'll cross that bridge when we come to it,' he said firmly. 'As for you—well, you can attend surgeries and clients will understand. Janey won't mind—she's a good-natured girl. Then, of course, you can come out with me on my calls—which will be nice for me.' He smiled at her so warmly that she felt a surge of gratitude towards him.

She said, 'I might have known you would help me out. You came to us like an answer to a prayer when my mother and I were at our wits' end and now—' she shrugged '—I can't find words to express what I feel.'

'Neither can I.' He looked at her steadily for a few moments, then turned to Mrs Norton who was clearing away the remains of a meal she had hastily assembled for them both. 'I think Alice ought to go to bed, don't you?'

She nodded. 'I'll see that she does.' She laughed gently. 'What's more, I'm beginning to think this accident may be a blessing in disguise. A good rest from work—just what she needs. Thank goodness you and Janey are here.'

Getting ready for bed, Alice found everything more difficult than she had anticipated. Taking off her clothes was bad enough and dressing, no doubt, would be worse. It was incredible how such a small injury could change one's everyday life.

After an uncomfortable night she began to find ways of dealing with difficulties as they presented themselves and for a short time she wondered if she might be able to cope with working in the surgery. But her mother quickly disillusioned her.

'You really have to accept that you're out of action for a while. Look—' she pointed to the window '—here comes Janey. James must have persuaded her to help out. She'll want you to show her what's what in the surgery.'

Janey came in, cheerfully accepted a coffee and, after expressing her sympathy, she said, 'Well, it's bad luck for you but good luck for me. I've been dying to do some work in an English practice. So don't worry. Your veterinary nurse and I will keep things ticking over till you're fit again, to say nothing of James who will continue to keep the farmers sweet.'

Alice stared. 'I thought you had to go back to Australia in about a fortnight's time?'

'Think I'd let you down like that? No, I'll stay on till your wrist is healed.' She grinned. 'No need to look so surprised. All that business with James's father's practice can wait. James and I have talked it over and we're both agreed that his old man will just have to be patient.'

Alice's spirits lifted to an almost incredible height. From then on she put up with all the inconveniences with a light heart and contented herself with staying in the background while Janey dealt very competently with all the work that came in.

Occasionally she would consult Alice as to treatment for a difficult case and that was nice but gradually she realised that she could leave the small animals safely in Janey's and Carol's capable hands.

At the end of the week James asked if she would like to go out on a call with him.

'I've got to see one of Mr Parker's cows. It hasn't responded to the usual antibiotics so I'm treating it with a new drug. It seems to be working. Mr Parker had no faith in it at first but now he's coming round, albeit rather grudgingly.'

As they drove off he said, 'You've been very

good about that wrist. No moaning or self-pity.'

Alice warmed to his praise and said impulsively, 'Actually I think it's a bit of a blessing. It has meant a kind of holiday for me.'

'Yes,' he said drily, 'and a complete change of plans all round.'

Instantly she was repentant. 'Oh, dear, I'm sorry. I was only thinking of myself. Have you heard from your father? Does it mean that you've missed your opportunity?'

'What opportunity? No need to answer—I know what you mean. But I never intended to take up his offer. The only thing I shall do is to help Janey out financially. She's a good girl and deserves to get on. She says she would like me to share the practice with her and her boyfriend but that's out of the question.'

'Why?' Alice looked at him curiously and saw his mouth tighten. She added quickly, 'Sorry, I suppose I shouldn't ask.'

'Good God!' His voice was harsh. 'Don't you understand yet?'

Confused, she shook her head. 'No, I don't understand. How can I be expected to know what's going on in your mind?'

'Or I in yours. How can I say what I want to when you have made it plain that our future partnership—if it comes off—must be based on a purely platonic arrangement? You obviously have no feelings for me other than that of a colleague.'

Stunned, Alice sat in silence. She was still searching for words when he added grimly, 'I know it's no use, so forget what I said.' He changed the subject. 'We mustn't be late for Mr Parker.'

The next half-hour passed in a kind of daze for Alice. Standing in the cowshed listening to James praising the new treatment, she found it hard to concentrate as he examined his patient. Tactfully he said to Mr Parker, 'It's only worked because you've followed my directions implicity. Most farmers would have given up by now and insisted on sending this animal in to the knackers.'

Mr Parker beamed. 'Well, I'm not against progress. That heifer is valuable. I didn't want to lose her. I just hope your bill won't be too high.'

James grinned. 'Not much more than you would have got for her carcass. Much more profit to you than to us.'

After a few more words of advice from James they parted on good terms. James laughed ruefully as they drove out of the farmyard.

'These farmers—they only look on their animals as investments, whereas we try to spare them suffering and our satisfaction is in every life saved.'

Alice nodded in agreement and once more silence descended. Her thoughts were confused. She desperately wanted more of an explanation from him but felt instinctively that this was not the time or the place to try to get him to open up. A glimmer of light was flickering in her troubled mind but she dared not dwell on it for fear that that tremulous hope might be crushed.

His voice broke the silence. 'One more call.

Sophie has a nanny-goat she'd like me to examine—it's due to kid soon. She also asked me to bring you with me for coffee or tea.'

He glanced at the car clock. 'Three thirty—well, tea seems to be indicated.' He glanced at her questioningly. 'Say yes, will you? Personally I'm parched and Sophie will put on a more interesting tea than we will find in the surgery.'

Alice smiled. 'Yes, willingly. I'd like to see Sophie again. And perhaps we'll see the children.'

He grinned ruefully. 'They're nice kids but they're little devils at times. Like all children, I suppose. It's a very happy family. I envy them.' As he turned the car in the direction of his brother's house he added quietly, 'They're still very much in love.'

'You sound surprised. Don't you believe in a lasting love?'

He shrugged. 'I used to but I've found it's easy to make a mistake.' He paused. 'My fiancée, for instance. I thought I really loved her but when I found out she was unfaithful my love died instantly. I ought to have been heartbroken, whereas I was furious at first and then vastly relieved.'

He stopped the car at the first gate of the long drive but before he got out to open it he added quietly, 'Since then, I've fallen in love so deeply that I realise the other was only a sham. But if this one comes to nothing there'll never be anyone else.'

Alice could feel her heart beating wildly. She longed to ask the vital question but her courage failed. She might very well receive an answer that would crush that small glimmer of hope at the back of her mind.

Still deliberating, she realised that he had got out to open the gate and had driven through. As he returned from shutting it he gave her a long searching look and settled down to drive up to his brother's farm.

What did that look mean? It might well be, she told herself, that he was telling her not to build up her hopes or that he wanted her to ask him to elaborate further.

Her faint hope suddenly faded. She had no reason to imagine that he was referring to her—she was deluding herself again. But then who could it be? It certainly wasn't Becky, so—all at once her heart sank. Janey, yes, that was more than likely. He was always praising her and, of course, living in the same house it seemed almost inevitable. Her fears were strengthened later on when Sophie pointed to a farm cat strolling across the yard.

'She got torn on some barbed wire last week—a nasty gash—and as you two were not around I asked Janey to deal with her.' She turned to James. 'If you remember, when you came back that evening you admired what you called her "needlework".' She paused.

'She tells me she is hoping to take over your father's practice but that it all depends on you.' For a moment she looked at him quizzically. 'Come on, brother-in-law, what's going on between you?'

Alice's heart sank even further. Pretending indifference, she moved away, but not out of earshot, and heard him laugh.

'My dear Sophie, you've got the wrong end of the stick again. I'm sure if there was anything between Janey and me she would have confided in you. As it is, I believe she has a steady relationship with a boyfriend in Perth. He rings up regularly and is very anxious for her to return.'

'Oh, dear.' Sophie shrugged ruefully. 'Wrong again! Well—come and see Gilda. I can't be mistaken there—she's due to kid soon and I'm sure it's imminent.'

James laughed. 'You can never be quite sure with nanny-goats. I remember making a fool of myself once, some time ago, when I was called in because the owner said her goat was due to kid that day. After examining her I said very confidently that as the gestation period—about a hundred and fifty days—wasn't up it wouldn't happen for another three or four days.

'Fifteen minutes after I'd left the house the wretched animal had two kids very quickly and I felt a complete idiot.'

Leading them to a block of outhouses, Sophie pointed Gilda out.

'There she is, peering over the door. Isn't she sweet? She's so affectionate and when I take her outside she follows me round like a dog. She knows her name too.' As soon as Sophie went up to her, Gilda reared herself up on her hind legs and laid her head gently on her owner's shoulder. Stroking her lovingly, Sophie said, 'She's a bit hot. Do you think she's got a temperature?'

James took out a thermometer, inserted it and stood waiting for the requisite time. Withdrawing it, he frowned. 'You're right. It's quite high. I'll give her an injection now and another one tomorrow.

'Now, as regards this imminent event—' Going into the box, he began a careful examination. At last he shook his head. 'I'm pretty sure—' he laughed '—as sure as anyone can be that she won't kid for about another week. There you are—I've laid my head on the block. I may be wrong, of course, and just in case I am you'll have to keep a close watch on her.'

'So will you,' Sophie retorted, 'and if I should prove to be right you'll never hear the last of it.'

Laughing together, they went into the house and as they entered the kitchen Alice gasped in admiration at the sight of a magnificent fruit cake in the centre of the table. Sophie said proudly, 'I may get a lot of facts wrong but in cookery I don't make mistakes.'

James said penitently, 'I apologise for seeming to put you down. You mustn't take it to heart. You're a wonderful wife and mother and I reckon that's worth more than anything.'

Sophie laughed. 'It's usually despised nowadays but David and the children are happy and that's all that matters to me.'

Alice smiled. 'I should say you're worth at least two men when I think of all the work you have to do in this big house with the farm and two children—by the way, where are they?'

'Oh, they're on a school outing. They won't be in till late so let's make the most of a little peace.'

Seated at the well-scrubbed kitchen table, the conversation was general at first and, after condoling with Alice over her broken wrist, Sophie brought up the subject of Janey once more.

Turning to James, she said, 'You say she has a boyfriend but from what she has told me she isn't heavily involved. If you ask me—and I don't think I'm wrong about this—she would like you to take on your father's practice and employ her as an assistant with a view to eventual partnership. She's even hinted that she would like me to find out what you think of that idea.'

Alice tried to control her involuntary gasp of dismay but from the lightning glance James shot at her she realised that he had seen her reaction. Instead of answering Sophie, he merely shrugged. Taking a slice of cake, he bit into it. 'Lovely cake. Clever Sophie.'

'Don't be so evasive.' His sister-in-law was irritated. 'I want to know what you think of Janey's idea.'

'It all depends,' he said briefly and went on eating with obvious pleasure while Sophie glared at him.

Turning to Alice, she said hopelessly, 'He's utterly impossible to pin down, isn't he? How do you manage to deal with him?'

Aware that his eyes were on her, she forced a laugh. 'He's a law unto himself. I've given up trying to understand him.'

It was when they were driving back that James

broke the silence. 'If you will come out with me one evening I'll explain why I'm so difficult to, as Sophie says, "pin down".'

In spite of her fast-beating heart she managed to say sceptically, 'You've said that before but if you remember you didn't get far. Veterinary interference—it was a horse with colic, wasn't it?'

He nodded ruefully. 'There's always that, of course.' He paused for a few moments, then suddenly said, 'I've got it. I'll get Peter Wood—you know, the vet over at Summerhill—to stand in for me for a whole day. We'll leave the surgery to Janey and Carol and we can then be free to go off somewhere—the sea perhaps—where no one can call me out. You could certainly do with a change of scenery, couldn't you?'

Alice's spirits rose miraculously. A day out with him—whatever the outcome—would at least be a memory to treasure. They began to discuss on which specific day to go, but James said, 'Leave it to me. I'll fix it all up.' He went on, 'We'd better make it soon so that we can take advantage of this present spell of good weather.'

Two days later Alice woke to a perfect morning and the prospect of spending it in James's company filled her with joy. No matter where they went or what they did, the fact that they would be entirely on their own was enough.

He came for her soon after breakfast and in his casual clothes he looked so handsome that her heart seemed to melt with love. She herself had dressed with difficulty, hindered by her plastered wrist, but in beige trousers, a cream silk shirt, a wide leather belt emphasising her slim waist and her beautiful hair held in control by a velvet bandeau, she knew she looked her best.

He said nothing but his eyes showed his appreciation and there was something in that look that made her pulses race. Settled in his car, she sighed with pleasure and he glanced at her quickly.

'Why the sigh? Don't you want to come?'

She laughed. 'You're like Sophie. You've got me wrong. It was a sigh of relief at leaving all my cares behind me. Don't you feel the same?'

He nodded. 'I certainly do but my pleasure is mixed with apprehension.' He stopped and waited as though he expected her to ask for an explanation but a sudden chill enveloped her. Was he dreading telling her that he had decided to return to Australia?

At last she said, 'I'm apprehensive too so let's get the talking over and then we can enjoy the rest of the day.'

To her dismay he shook his head. 'This is not the time or place.' He paused. 'Shall we take this road to the coast? It's warm enough to sit on the beach. I've got a picnic hamper in the back. Sophie made it up this morning and, knowing her, it's sure to be good. I've also put in a bottle of wine—Australian, of course—but I'll have to limit myself to the legal amount.'

Once more the chill came over her at the mention of Australia but all she said was, 'Yes. I'd love to go the sea.'

After a short period of searching they found a quiet bay in the shelter of the cliffs. Placing the hamper on the ground, he looked around. 'Absolutely deserted. Perfect.'

Alice settled herself on the rug he spread out and drew in a long breath of the salty air. The tide was going out and gradually exposing blue-green rocks which glistened in the sunshine. The only sounds came from the seagulls circling round the cliffs. Suddenly Alice had a flash of premonition. This scene would stay in her mind for the rest of her life—for it was here that her fate was going to be decided.

She heard James say, 'An early lunch, I think. Let's see what Sophie has given us.'

He drew out two Thermos flasks filled with what proved to be delicious herby soup, then a choice of home-made pâté or salami with crusty bread followed by what James called the main course—chicken drumsticks coated in breadcrumbs and Parmesan cheese.

They also found an interesting mixed salad and a tempting chocolate mousse rounded it all off. They both set to with a will, the lovely surroundings contributing to their enjoyment of the spread set before them. Eventually Alice lay back on the rug, beyond further culinary temptation. She shook her head and laughed at James, who was still eating with obvious enjoyment. 'Not another thing or I shall fall asleep.'

'Don't do that,' he said in false alarm. 'We have to talk. At least I have to do some explaining. But first I must have your answer to a question that will change my whole life.'

She gave an involuntary shiver and half turned

away but his voice was suddenly stern. 'No, don't try to dodge it. You must give me a truthful answer.' He paused, drew a long breath and said quietly, 'Alice, I want to know how you would feel if I went back to Australia permanently to take over my father's practice. Would you feel only a brief regret which would soon be forgotten once you had found someone to replace me?'

Shocked, she turned to face him and found herself speechless. He was putting her at a disadvantage. How could she answer truthfully without betraying her love for him? At last she said, 'How can I answer that? It's too difficult.'

'Just the same, I must know. Please—don't torment me.'

He took her by the shoulders and she saw such pleading in his eyes that she took her courage in both hands. She said steadily, 'If you go back to Australia it will break my heart.'

'Oh! Thank God!' He jumped to his feet and pulled her up with him. The next moment she was folded in his arms and he was raining kisses on her face. Pressed up against him she could feel his heart beating as wildly as her own. Then, seeking her mouth, he kissed her so passionately that she felt she would faint with ecstasy.

Loosening his hold, he looked deeply into her eyes. His voice was broken and he shook his head in bewilderment. 'I can scarcely believe it. Darling, darling Alice—do you really love me? Is it possible that you love me as much as I love you?'

She smiled mischievously. 'How do I know how

much you love me? You've made me break all
the rules and tell you first.'

'Break what rules? My darling, there aren't any
rules where love is concerned.' He paused. 'Alice,
I love you, adore you and I'll do my best to make
you as happy as you've made me.' He drew her
close again and for the next few minutes they
were locked in a mutual passion that grew to such
intensity that at last, gasping for breath, Alice
lowered her head and laid it on his chest.

Suddenly, gently, he laid her down on the rug.
Looking up at him she saw the question in his
eyes. It was plain to read and when he asked
softly, 'Now?' she hesitated for a long moment.
He smiled down at her. 'You'd rather wait?'

She nodded and stroked his cheek. 'Do
you mind?'

'Yes and no.' His eyes were tender. 'If you
prefer to wait then I will.' He gave a little laugh.
'With difficulty.' Then very seriously he asked,
'How long will I have to wait?'

She said nothing and at last he smiled. 'I'll
answer that myself.' Tracing his fingers along the
line of her throat, he asked very quietly, 'Darling
Alice, will you marry me?'

It was only when she heard the actual words
that she realised how much she had been afraid
that marriage was not in his mind. Her eyes must
have reflected her relief for he said, 'You surely
didn't think that I meant anything other than
marriage?'

She hesitated again and said a little nervously,
'Well, after your previous bad experience—'

'Ah! That!' He took her up quickly. 'I admit it made me feel that I daren't trust myself with any woman again. But that was when I had a burden of guilt on my back. Having fallen in love with you so quickly, I felt I had to fight against it. Into the bargain, you seemed only interested in your ambition to hold onto your practice and looked upon me as a mere stopgap for six months.

'Admit, my sweet darling, that you gave me no encouragement at all.'

She smiled up at him mistily. 'True. I was afraid that you wanted to take over my practice. Then, as I realised I had fallen in love with you, your father's offer came up and I grew terrified that you would go back to Australia.'

He nodded. 'I played with the idea because I thought I hadn't a hope in hell that you would ever care for me. But now you've made me the happiest man on earth—to settle down in my own country with you as my wife—' His voice broke and he buried his face in her hair.

Suddenly a thought seemed to strike him and, lifting his head, he said, 'But I'm being selfish. Perhaps you would like to go to Australia and share my father's practice with me?'

Startled, Alice sat up and stared at him. 'Well, I'd love to go there one day just to visit but—' She shook her head slowly. Then hastily she added, 'Of course, if you want to, then it's OK with me.'

'My lovely darling.' He took her once more into his arms and laughed gently. 'That is really too much. Do you think I want such a docile wife?'

She leant back and looked him in the face. 'I just want to let you know that I'll be happy with you wherever we live.' She paused. 'A docile wife?' Laughingly she traced the outline of his face. 'No. Ours will be a partnership. Signed, sealed and binding for ever.'

He crushed her to him and she yielded in an ecstasy of love, knowing that all misunderstandings had been resolved. This man—this wonderful man—who had come to her for what was to be a limited period had changed her whole life and would be her true love for always.

MILLS & BOON®

Something new and exciting is happening to...

Medical Romance™

From August 1996, the covers will change to a stylish new white design which will certainly catch your eye!

They're the same Medical Romance™ stories we know you enjoy, we've just improved their look.

4 titles published every month at £2.10 each

MILLS & BOON®

Back by Popular Demand

BETTY NEELS

COLLECTOR'S EDITION

A collector's edition of favourite titles from one of the world's best-loved romance authors.

Mills & Boon are proud to bring back these sought after titles, now reissued in beautifully matching volumes and presented as one cherished collection.

Don't miss these unforgettable titles, coming next month:

Title #7   THE MOON FOR LAVINIA
Title #8   PINEAPPLE GIRL

Available wherever
Mills & Boon books are sold

MILLS & BOON®

From Here To Paternity

Don't miss our great new series featuring
fantastic men who eventually make
fabulous fathers.

Some seek paternity, some have it thrust
upon them—all will make it—whether
they like it or not!

In August '96, look out for:

Grounds for Marriage
by Daphne Clair

GET 4 BOOKS
AND A MYSTERY GIFT

Return this coupon and we'll send you 4 Medical Romance™ novels and a mystery gift absolutely FREE! We'll even pay the postage and packing for you.

We're making you this offer to introduce you to the benefits of Reader Service: FREE home delivery of brand-new Medical Romance novels, at least a month before they are available in the shops, FREE gifts and a monthly Newsletter packed with information.

Accepting these FREE books and gift places you under no obligation to buy, you may cancel at any time, even after receiving just your free shipment. Simply complete the coupon below and send it to:

MILLS & BOON® READER SERVICE, FREEPOST, CROYDON, SURREY, CR9 3WZ.

No stamp needed

Yes, please send me 4 free Medical Romance novels and a mystery gift. I understand that unless you hear from me, I will receive 4 superb new titles every month for just £2.10* each postage and packing free. I am under no obligation to purchase any books and I may cancel or suspend my subscription at any time, but the free books and gifts will be mine to keep in any case. (I am over 18 years of age)

2EP6D

Ms/Mrs/Miss/Mr _____

Address _____

_____

_____ Postcode _____

MILLS & BOON®

Medical Romance™

Books for enjoyment this month...

A PRIVATE AFFAIR	Sheila Danton
DOCTORS IN DOUBT	Drusilla Douglas
FALSE PRETENCES	Laura MacDonald
LOUD AND CLEAR	Josie Metcalfe

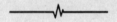 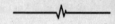

Treats in store!

Watch next month for these absorbing stories...

ONE STEP AT A TIME	Caroline Anderson
VET WITH A SECRET	Mary Bowring
DEMI'S DIAGNOSIS	Lilian Darcy
A TIME TO CHANGE	Maggie Kingsley